ROAD KILL

A ZOMBIE TALE

OTHER BOOKS BY ANTHONY GIANGREGORIO

THE DEAD WATER SERIES

DEADWATER
DEADWATER: Expanded Edition
DEADRAIN
DEADCITY
DEADWAVE
DEAD HARVEST
DEAD UNION
DEAD VALLEY

ALSO BY THE AUTHOR

DEAD RECKONING: DAWNING OF THE DEAD
THE MONSTER UNDER THE BED
DEAD END: A ZOMBIE NOVEL
DEAD TALES: SHORT STORIES TO DIE FOR
DEAD MOURNING: A ZOMBIE HORROR STORY
DEADFREEZE
DEADFALL
DEADRAGE
SOUL-EATER
THE DARK
RISE OF THE DEAD
DARK PLACES

ROAD KILL

A ZOMBIE TALE

ANTHONY GIANGREGORIO

ROAD KILL: A ZOMBIE TALE

Copyright © 2009 by Anthony Giangregorio

ISBN   Softcover ISBN 13: 978-1-935458-12-8
                        ISBN 10: 1-935458-12-4

This is a work of fiction. Names, characters, places and incidents either are the product of the author's imagination or are used fictitiously, and any resemblance to any actual persons, living or dead, events, or locales is entirely coincidental.

This book was printed in the United States of America.

For more info on obtaining additional copies of this book, contact:
www.livingdeadpress.com

ACKNOWLEDGMENTS

Thanks to my wife Jody for all her support and reading all my work (even when she gets tired of it), and to my son, Joseph, who helps more than he realizes.
Also, my son, Domenic, who always has a new idea and a creative way to kill a zombie. And to Marc Wiggins, for his contribution to this book.

AUTHOR'S NOTE

This book was self-edited, and though I tried my absolute best to correct all grammar mistakes; there may be a few here and there.
Please accept my sincerest apology for any errors you may find.

This is the second edition of this book.

Visit my web site at undeadpress.com

1

BEGINNINGS

INTERSTATE 495 STRETCHED for miles in each direction, the empty highway making the lone woman walking on the shoulder feel like she was the last person on Earth.

Above her head, the amber, sun-dappled sky was marred with white, fluffy clouds. A few were tinted with black, signifying the coming of a storm.

All around her was nothing but forest, the oaks and maples, interspersed with a few pines, covering miles and miles of New Hampshire woodland.

Wiping her brow, not wanting the small trickle of sweat to crease her makeup, she gazed up into the still slightly azure sky, noticing the odd yellow tint to the horizon.

She knew why that odd color was there, though she wasn't very interested.

A rogue comet was approaching the planet Earth and the comet's tail would easily be seen when the Earth was swallowed inside it. But all the astronomy experts and scientists believed there would be no harm, just a glorious light show for the people of Earth to enjoy.

With a weary sigh, she gazed back down towards Earth, towards the lonely blacktop.

Looking behind her, she could see the waves of heat emanating off the highway and then, as if appearing magically, a small spot appeared.

Bethany Wheeler's eyes opened wider and her heart began beating faster in expectation of the growing object. Her feet were killing her and she desperately wanted a ride. She was at the point now where she would take a ride from anyone, even if they did look a little creepy.

With each passing second the object grew larger until the classic shape of an old Cadillac coupe de ville appeared. It was lipstick red with a white hardtop, and the hubcaps flashed silver in the sun. Bethany turned to the car and waved, her backpack feeling heavy on her shoulders.

She was rewarded for her effort when the Cadillac tooted its deep horn, and then began to pull over to the side of the road, the front bumper coming within inches of her legs. With a smile and a hop, Beth ran to the passenger door, the driver of the Caddy still unknown, as the windshield reflected the sunlight so she couldn't penetrate the glass with her gaze.

Upon reaching the door, she bent over and peered into the interior. It smelled of old sweat and fast food; and something else. At first she couldn't place the scent and then her nose picked out the other odor amidst the half dozen others. It was the fake scent of pine, and sure enough, her gaze went to the little pine freshener hanging from the rearview mirror, the small green cutout swinging back and forth like a tiny pendulum. She found that amusing as all around her the real scent of pine filled the highway.

Her attention was then drawn to the driver as he shifted position on the red leather seats and flashed a smile that quickly put off her defensive nature when meeting a potential ride.

He was a pudgy man in his late fifties with little hair and a day's worth of stubble.

Where his chin once was, there were now two, the lower one wagging whenever he would talk. His eyes were deep set behind a heavy face, which matched the man's round beer belly. Stubby fingers gripped the steering wheel and two of them were adorned with rings. A Bible lay on the front seat next to him, half open near his chubby leg.

But it wasn't the smile so much as the white collar he wore around his neck and the large silver cross hanging below it which had her lowering her guard.

"Well, hello there, little lady. Looks like you could use a ride. May I offer you one?"

Bethany nodded, shifting her backpack off her shoulder.

"That would be great, ah, reverend is it?"

He shook his head. "Not a reverend, little lady, a pastor." He opened his right hand wide and spread his arm across the seat. "Pastor Martin James at your service; formerly of the Church of Christ out of Boston."

Beth opened the door, dropped her backpack into the rear seat and climbed inside. Upon sitting, she turned and flashed Pastor James a smile of her own.

"Hi, I'm Bethany."

Pastor James pulled back onto the highway and continued on. "Pleased to meet you, Bethany. And where's a pretty little thing like you headed?"

"Maine, I'm going to see my sister."

He nodded slightly. "And you plan on hitchhiking the entire way?"

She nodded, leaned back, and let the warm air flowing in through the windows dry the perspiration from her face.

"You bet. Hitchhiked all the way from Florida and I'm finally almost there."

Pastor James shook his head. "But don't you worry about getting in the wrong car? There's a lot of immoral souls out there in the world."

Beth shrugged. "Yeah, I guess, but I'd like to think I'm a good judge of character. I don't go with anyone I think is a creep."

Pastor James grinned. "So, does that mean I pass the test?"

Beth chuckled, and nodded. "Sure does, I mean if I can't trust a man of God then who can you trust, right?" She closed her eyes then and let the breeze cascade over her.

"Indeed," Pastor James said as he let his eyes roam over Beth's legs and follow the lines to the juncture of her thighs. With her eyes closed, she never knew of the man of God's lecherous gaze.

With the sky slowly tinting a darker yellow with each passing second, the comet drew nearer, while the red Cadillac sped down the lonely highway.

* * *

"Order Up!" A woman's voice screeched through the head-high turnstile separating the kitchen from the main floor of DJ's truck stop and diner just off Exit 9 of Interstate 495.

Out in the patched parking lot were five rigs, three family sedans, two Ford trucks, and an old pickup truck filled with fertilizer that should have been put out to pasture during Reagan's turn in office.

It was just past noon and the lunch rush had just ended, leaving only a few weary truck drivers and a few families heading north to Maine.

"Did you hear me, Jake? I said order up!" Mary Jane hollered for the second time.

There was movement in the kitchen, but with the turnstile in the way she couldn't see what was happening back there. Yes, she could bend over and look through the opening where the food was placed when it was prepared, but that would mean she would have to bend over and her back wouldn't like that very much. Mary Jane was in her late sixties but her back felt like it was in her late eighties. A lot of it had to do with the ponderous breasts she carried on a daily basis.

At twenty two years old, the mammoth breasts had been glorious, and every woman in the county had been envious, but now in her late sixties, they were nothing but a nuisance. And her bra strap was killing her. She couldn't wait to get home tonight and take the damn thing off. Looking around in frustration, she tried to peer past the turnstile. There was a small bell near the shelf and she slapped it three times.

"Hello, in there! Damn it, Jake, where the hell are you?"

Suddenly a head popped out of the shelf near her belly and a young man's face was staring up at her. She had to shift back slightly so she could see him, as her breasts were blocking her line of sight.

"Hey, Mary Jane, you called? I was in the back room stocking the shelves while it's been slow. We used a lot of stuff from the lunch rush." His eyes stared at her large chest and he grinned. "I swear, those things get bigger every day. What're you feedin' 'em."

Mary Jane scowled as she gazed down at Jake, the fry cook and all around pain in the ass of the diner. But she had to admit he was cute and if she was thirty years younger she was fairly confident he and her would have spent at least one night in the back room together. With a weary sigh, she shook her head. Those days were gone, at least for her.

"Now you stop it, Jake, or so help me, I'll slap you silly."

Jake grinned lecherously. Mary Jane may have been in her sixties, but she had kept her figure and her face was still attractive, despite the crow's feet and laugh lines.

"I'm sorry, what's up?"

Mary Jane pointed to the turnstile. "You've got an order up. Grilled cheese and a side of fries."

Nodding, he slid out of the shelf and plucked the paper from the turnstile. "Be up in a minute!" He called through the shelf to Mary Jane.

She nodded and turned away to see to her other customers. Walking around the counter, she deftly picked up the coffee pot near the end and strolled over to the first booth lining the glass walls of the diner.

A small man in his late forties with no hair on top and a pair of thin glasses cropped on his nose was staring into a book. When Mary Jane drew closer, she paused, looking over the man's shoulder. It was a book with pictures of birds in it, and when she read a few of the names to herself, she realized most were indigenous to New Hampshire.

"Bird watcher, huh?" She asked while offering him a refill of coffee. He gestured to his cup and she poured while he began chatting.

"Oh my, yes. There are simply so many wonderful species to see here in New England. I've driven down from New York State to see them."

Mary Jane nodded, not amused. This guy drove all the way from New York to look at a bunch of birds. She wanted to ask what the deal was. Weren't there enough birds in New York to keep him happy, but she bit her tongue. He was a tourist after all and tourists brought in money.

"That's great, well, good luck," she said pleasantly and moved away to the next booth.

This one had a young couple, no more than twenty-five years old each. They were talking softly and were sitting next to one another. The man's hand was lost under the table and Mary Jane grinned. Ah youth. She remembered quite a few hidden hands when she was younger and was playing the field.

"Coffee folks?"

"Nah, thanks, miss, but we're good," the man said while the woman giggled, trying to control herself.

"Matt, will you stop? We're in a public place," she said in a hushed voice.

"And that's what makes it so much fun, Liz," he answered back and proceeded to make her squirm.

Mary Jane chuckled and move to the next booth. This one was empty so she continued on.

The next booth had another couple in it, as well, though where the other couple was young and full of life; these two were tired and worn out. Neither talked while they poked around the daily special and Mary Jane cleared her throat to get their attention.

"Coffee?"

"Yes, please, I'd love another cup," the man said.

"Don't you think you've had enough, Walter? You know what all that caffeine does to you, especially when you have to sit in the car for so long," the woman said in a dry voice.

The man sighed. "Of course I know, Ruth, why do you think I want some more? Christ, we've got another three hours of driving before we get to your mother's house, don't you think I need to stay awake?"

"Well, I could talk to you," she said as if that settled everything.

Walter made a disgusted noise with his lips and pushed his empty coffee cup to the edge of the table.

"No thank you, I think I'll stick with the coffee." Reading her signal, Mary Jane poured him a fresh cup.

They began to bicker back and forth and Mary Jane poured the coffee and stepped away. She knew their type. Married for twenty years and the marriage had ended fifteen ago, but both were too stubborn to admit it to one another.

Heading to the next booth, she smiled at the three truckers.

She knew all three men. They were regulars who drove past her diner almost every month. They would always chat with her and she would flirt with them. Bubba was the first man sitting behind the table, his generous girth barely crammed behind the Formica. He had a thick red beard and matching mane of hair and his grin was wide as hell when she approached.

"Well, there's my favorite gal, I thought you'd forgotten me," Bubba said with a twinkle in his eye.

She grinned back and poured more coffee into the cup Bubba held in his hand. He was a regular and knew the drill.

"Oh, please, she probably tried to forget you the second she was through taking your order," the second man said. His name was Wilson and he was a skinny guy who looked like the wind would blow him away with the first heavy gust. But he was a veteran truck driver and despite belaying the heavy set look of almost every trucker who entered the diner, he knew his trade.

"You're just jealous of him, that's all. Hell, you're jealous of all of us what with that toothpick of a frame you're sportin'." This came from the other man sitting next to him. Bubba got his own side of the table because he was too big to let anyone sit with him.

"Very, funny, Wilbur," Wilson said with a frown. "We can't all be size sixty waists, ya know."

"That's fifty-seven and half, if you must know," Wilbur spat back.

Bubba chuckled, a deep resonance that made him sound like Santa Claus. "Well, Wilson, maybe if you ate something once in a while you'd gain some weight."

Bubba illustrated his point by taking a bite out of the massive hamburger on his plate, the grease slipping down the sides of his mouth to drip back onto the plate.

Wilson turned away, disgusted. "God, Bubba, I don't know how you can eat that stuff. Do you even know how many growth hormones and chemicals they pump into that meat before it gets to your plate?"

Bubba shook his head and took another bite, and with his mouth full of food, he smiled. "It's the growth hormones that make it so sweet."

Wilson turned away, and turned to Mary Jane. "Maybe you can talk some sense into him, Mary Jane. He's killing himself with every bite he takes."

Mary Jane shrugged. "Sorry, honey, you're preachin' to the wrong choir. He's my best customer. Whatever he wants to eat is fine with me."

She filled the other two cups and shuffled away while Wilson and the other two men continued arguing over the rights of beef and Wilson' skinny frame.

Wandering to the counter, she saw her grilled cheese was ready. Picking up the plate, she grabbed a napkin and ketchup and carried it to the last patron of the diner this afternoon.

She was a petite woman, five-five was a good guess, maybe twenty years old with soft brown hair, and her attention was focused in a book similar to the one the Birdman had. She barely looked up when Mary Jane set the plate down.

"There you go, honey, anything else?"

She shook her head. "No thanks, I'm fine."

Mary Jane frowned, knowing when she was being dismissed, and though it was the life of a waitress, she still had never liked it. Turning on her heels, she walked away. She bet the tip would suck, too.

With all her customers taken care of for the time being, she moved to the counter and picked up the remote for the TV and turned up the volume. A news reporter was standing in a grass field, while he gestured up to the sky with his right hand. Even with the old, color television set she could see the sky was a bright yellow, the white and grey clouds standing out drastically.

"I'm standing here on the outskirts of Portsmouth, near the junction for I-95, and from here I think you the viewers can see just how amazing the horizon is thanks to the coming of Halfort's Comet. Now, for those of you who don't follow astronomy, Professor Cornelius Halfort discovered this rogue comet more than fifty years ago and predicted its arrival back in 1958. As you can see by the sky, the Earth has been inside the comet's tail for almost six hours and it is estimated we will remain in the tail for at least another two full days. When the second day is over, the comet will be free of Earth's gravity and will continue further into our galaxy on an incredibly long orbit around our sun. It is estimated the comet won't return for more than two-hundred years, so all of us alive to witness this spectacular event should be thankful, as it will be future generations who will witness its return.

If you look up at the sky, you will see the yellow tint. Scientists have theorized this is an effect of the comet, due to its high content of radioactive metals, but fear not, we here on Earth are perfectly safe. I repeat, there is no reason to panic, just enjoy the light show for the next forty-eight hours. This is James Balasco, for WGWN News, New Hampshire."

"Hey, Mary Jane, how 'bout a refill!" One of the truckers called.

"Huh? Oh, sure, coming right up," she said and reached for the coffee pot. She made a note to start a fresh pot.

Pressing the mute button on the television, she turned toward the truckers, then paused for a moment, leaning down and gazing through the opening that led into the kitchen.

"Hey, Jake, how 'bout taking out the trash? It's been piling up for hours. You said you'd do it after the rush was over."

Jake's head appeared in the opening and he frowned.

"Yeah, I'll do it, hold your horses. First I gotta go see DJ."

"Fine, Jake, but as soon as you get back, you take the trash out, okay, hon?"

Jake grinned, that handsome grin that had Mary Jane feeling weak in the knees, though she would never tell the twenty year old man.

"For you, Mary Jane, anything." Then his head disappeared like a magic trick.

With a school girl grin on her face, Mary Jane headed into the diner to refill some coffee mugs.

* * *

Jake walked down the small hallway behind the kitchen until he reached the dirty and peeling-paint wooden door with the name D.J. Stubbs sprawled in black marker across the center of the middle panel.

Not relishing what his boss wanted, he knocked on the door.

There was a grunt of admission from the other side and he opened it. The room was small, only three times the size of a broom closet, but it served DJ well as an office.

Jake crossed the three feet until he was standing in front of the small wooden desk. DJ was reading some papers and Jake glanced at a few of them. It was the hourly wages for the employees at the diner.

DJ looked up at Jake, his eyes creasing into slits. Jake always thought DJ looked like the guy called Porky in the movie of the same name. He was a large man, but leaned more to fat than muscle. He had three chins and jowls that made him look like a bulldog. And to make the picture complete, he wore a large, white Stetson hat, like he was in Texas instead of New England. The faded brown suit he wore was covered in food stains from past meals, and if Jake looked close enough, the man's tie was a menu for the diner's daily specials.

"About time you got in here, I told Mary Jane I wanted to talk to you over an hour ago," DJ breathed heavily.

Jake shrugged. "Don't know what to tell you, DJ. She just told me a few minutes ago, guess she forgot, what with working by herself out there. You ever gonna get her some help?"

DJ snorted, the picture of a pig complete.

"Help? Shit, son, if anything I need to cut back. Which is why I wanted to talk to you. Listen, my profits are in the toilet and I'm afraid we all need to make some cutbacks; trim the fat so to speak. Starting with you and the other employees."

Jake frowned, not liking where this was going.

"What the hell are you talking about, DJ?"

DJ set the papers down and sighed, like what he was sharing with Jake was hard, like it was his very heart he was ripping out of his chest for the good of the diner. The act was only more false because of the flash of gold and diamonds on the mans hand's and below his chin; the large gold chain garish in its flamboyance as it swung back and forth between the two open buttons of his shirt.

"I'm saying I need to cut hours, but even if I do, there's still a lot of shit that needs to be done around here."

Jake nodded slightly. "Yeah, so, and that leads us to what exactly?"

DJ leaned forward, the chair under his ass creaking wearily.

"That means I need you and the others to clock out after seven hours, but still finish your eight hour shift."

Jake's eyes went wide when what DJ was telling him sunk in

"Are you fucking serious? Hell, no, screw you, DJ. I'm not working for free just so you can buy another Porsche or treat another hooker to a free ride until she dumps your fat ass."

DJ sat up, slapping his right hand on the desk top, then raising it and pointed it straight at Jake's face.

"Now, you just watch your mouth there, boy. And leave Candy out of this. She left because we weren't compatible, that's all."

Now it was Jake's turn to sneer. "Yeah, she wasn't compatible with your fat ass."

Jake was referring to Candy, a city hooker who DJ had met when he was in Portsmouth on business last month. The woman had milked him dry and had then picked up and left, leaving DJ with blue balls and an empty wallet. Behind his back, the entire diner teased him, but to his face everyone told him how sorry they were she'd left.

"You're pushing it, boy. All right, listen, I was gonna try and do this nicely, but screw you. You want it hard, fine then, here it is. From now on, you and the others will work for eight hours and punch out after seven. If you don't like it then get the hell out. Try and find another job around here. We both know it's either here, the chemical plant, or driving an hour and half to Portsmouth every day." He grinned malevolently. "So what's it gonna be?"

Jake scowled, his hands squeezing into fists by his sides. Dammit, the fat bastard was right. There were no jobs around here. Portsmouth was too far away for a commute, at least not at minimum wage, and the chemical plant was a death trap. He knew far too many people with lung problems from working there.

Whether he liked it or not, DJ had him and the other employees over a barrel. With a sigh and a growl, Jake nodded.

"Fine, you win, but this isn't over."

DJ chuckled, leaning back in his chair. A cigar appeared from a pocket and he rolled it in his stubby fingers.

"Oh, it's over, boy, and don't you forget it. Now get out of here and take out the damn trash. I can smell it from here."

Jake spun and crossed to the door, opening it, planning on slamming it good and hard.

"And one more thing, Jake."

Jake stopped, one hand on the door, his head slightly turned.

"I want you to tell the others about the new arrangement. Explain it to them so they get it, especially Carlos. He's been busting my balls for a raise for weeks. Like it my fault he has so many damn kids. Damn Spics, wear a condom for Christ sakes, it ain't rocket science!"

Jake didn't answer, but instead exited the office. His hand was on the door, ready to slam it, and at the last second he stopped. No, the fat bastard probably expected him to slam it. Instead, he closed it with a soft click.

Shaking his head at the injustices of the world; such as how a fat, prejudiced bastard like DJ was able to hold the lives of so many others in his chubby, sweaty hands; he moved down the small hallway to take out the trash.

Upon reaching the kitchen, he was surprised to see Mary Jane at the grill. She looked up as he entered and her face was one of overwork and exhaustion. She had been on since five a.m., as she had opened the diner, and she was looking forward to going home in a few hours. She was pushing a greasy burger across the grill as he moved up to her, ready to take the spatula from her hand.

"Its okay, honey, I got it. I know how to cook a burger after all. It's quiet out front. You go and take that trash out, okay?"

He rubbed against her, his arm brushing against the side of her left breast.

"Sure, Mary Jane, anything for you. I swear to God if I was twenty years older.

"Yeah, yeah, and if I was twenty years younger..." she left off. This was a common joke with the two of them, May-December flirting at its best. But the truth was she thought of Jake like a son and would never have considered doing anything illicit with him. Well, maybe for a second, but it was a quick second.

With a wise-ass smile on his handsome face, Jake moved away, gathering the trash and heading out the back to toss it into the waiting dumpster.

Upon stepping outside, he couldn't help but gaze up at the bright-yellow sky. The horizon, which would normally be an azure blue, was now as bright as a ripe banana; with rippling lines running through the golden glow. It reminded him of heat waves hovering over the highway in the middle of summer. Scratching his head at the cool looking effects, he crossed the side of the building until he reached the dumpster. He wasn't much for astronomy and could really give two damns about the comet passing by Earth a hundred and ten thousand miles away as it bathed his world with its brilliance.

The dumpster was closed and he propped one side open, then tossed the large trash bag over his shoulder. It landed with a resounding crash and was still. He was about to turn away, debating if he should take a cigarette break or get back inside and help Mary Jane, when he heard a strange mewling sound coming from behind the dumpster.

He paused, listening, wondering what it could be, and when he heard it again, he spun around to investigate. With slow footsteps, he circled the dumpster and halted as he gazed down the large rat with its head caught in one of DJ's rat traps. The fat man had put them there over a week ago to deter unwelcome rodents. As far as DJ was concerned, that was about as good as it would get for insect and rodent protection.

Jake stared fascinated while the rat struggled in the trap. Its head was securely trapped thanks to the strong steel bar which had snapped back, almost severing the rodent's neck from the rest of its body. Jake stared as the rat squirmed, trying to get free of its prison. Picking up a nearby pipe left over from some unknown construction, he poked the rat slightly, wanting to see what would happen. The rat went wild, its rear legs scratching at the dirt while the front legs tried to gain purchase, the rodent wanting to separate itself from the miniscule bear trap.

None of this made sense, Jake thought, while he continued to watch the twisting rodent. The spring bar had snapped its neck; that was clearly visible. The bar had sunk more than halfway into the fur and if Jake had thought he was somehow mistaken, then when the rat began pulling itself off the trap, he knew something wasn't right. With rear legs digging into the dirt, and front legs pushing off the trap, the rat began slowly separating itself from the bar. As it did this, the wound on its neck began to spread, until Jake could see the glistening blood seeping out. But there was something more. Now that he took another look, what he thought was just the rats movements was in fact hundreds, perhaps even a thousand, of maggots as they squirmed under the fur of the rodent, the black hair undulating like a living entity all its own.

And then it happened, though it defied everything Jake had ever learned in school and in the world.

The rat's head separated from its body. The rear half backed away from the trap, trailing bits of gristle and a trickle of dull red blood. Maggots spilled out of the open neck cavity and Jake felt his stomach churning within him.

The head remained trapped, the undead eyes blinking at nothing, but the headless rodent finished moving away from the trap and then turned to *stare* at Jake. The open neck was looking right at him, as if the rodent knew he was there.

It was an unsettling feeling, looking down on a headless rat which appeared to be still alive. The maggots continued feeding, oblivious to the locomotion of its food source. Jake couldn't help but stare dumbfounded.

The rats rear haunches seemed to tense, and the front legs flexed, and before Jake could do more than yelp in surprise, the headless rodent launched itself into the air, directly at his open mouth.

Instinct took over and Jake went back to his high school days, playing stick ball with his friends at Grover Field.

As the rat launched into the air, Jake swung the pipe like he was standing on home plate. The bar connected with the body of the rat, and the small animated cadaver exploded into a hundred gobbets of flesh. Maggots were sprayed everywhere and Jake could feel them crawling in his hair. A few went down the collar of his shirt. He ran away, running into the back lot, waving his hands like a madman, filled with an overwhelming feeling of absolute grossness.

His creepiness level was at a ten and he prayed that would be it.

Jumping up and down like a school girl who had been surprised by a spider, he shook his hair free and got any stray maggots out of his clothing. When he was finished, he moved back to the dumpster, his curiosity getting the better of him.

The rat was in so many pieces it was hard to make some of them out, but the few he saw were still twitching. A paw flicked as if it was trying to run, and a thigh flexed in anticipation of a jump that would ever come. A small heart, lying in the dirt still beat, and Jake's eyes went to the rat's head, still stuck in the trap. The dead eyes turned to stare at him and the small mouth opened. Nothing was emitted, thanks to the creature having no lungs to expel air with, but Jake could almost hear the silent screech in his head.

Raising one of his construction boots he had acquired from a past job high into the air, he stomped down hard on the head, flattening it to nothing but a bloody mess. Bits of brain and gore stuck to the sole of his boot and he dragged it on the ground, trying to wipe it free.

"Jesus, Christ, what the hell just happened here?" He muttered to himself, his voice sounding off kilter, like he needed to clear his throat or drink a glass of water.

Shaking his head, knowing there was definitely something off about what had just occurred, he reasoned there had to be a reasonable explanation.

Because if there wasn't, then he had just witnessed a zombie rat try to attack him, and that was down right ridiculous.

Rounding the building, he tossed the pipe away and reentered the diner, but if he had paused to glance out to the edge of the parking lot, where the woods encroached on the perimeter of the hardtop, he would have been shocked to see more than two dozen animals slinking out of the foliage, with hundreds more following.

All were dead, some by natural causes, some by hunters, and some by other predators who had fed on the carcasses and left the rest for scavengers.

The scientific reason for this to be happening was long and boring, but the simple fact was the dead animals of the world were rising, and it was soon to be like Wild Kingdom, but of the walking dead. Something in the comet's tail, a radioactive isotope perhaps, was somehow jump starting the inferior nervous systems of the dead animal's bodies and bringing them back to a state of life.

All over the globe, wherever a dead animal lay rotting, whether on a highway, in the sewer of New York, a field in Arizona, or in a family backyard in Maine, the dead wildlife of the earth was rising.

And the creatures were hungry for human flesh.

2

THE RISING IN EIGHT PARTS

New Haven, Connecticut

MICHELLE SHROEDER LEFT the living room, her daughter still sitting on the couch. She'd been crying.

Ten minutes ago, she had come to Michelle with tears in her eyes, sobbing about her pet gerbil, Mr. Tickles. It seemed Mr. Tickles had reached his life expectancy and had decided to die sometime in the afternoon.

After comforting her daughter, and trying to explain about life and death to a six-year-old, she had left the little girl on the couch, knowing she had a small cleanup job to attend to.

With a paper bag in hand, and a paper towel sheet for scooping Mr. Tickles up with, she entered her daughter's room with a heavy heart.

It was a shame, really. If Mr. Tickles had died while her daughter had been in school, she could have rushed to the pet store and picked up another one. Hell, the damn things all looked the same to her. She could have switched it out and had a new gerbil ready to go by the time her daughter returned home from school. But it wasn't to be and Michelle had ended up giving *the death speech* a little sooner than she had hoped.

The room was dim, the shade pulled down, and she flicked on the light, bathing the room in a pale glow. Walking to the window, she opened the shade, her eyes immediately going to the golden hue of the sky. She wasn't much interested in the comet, as she felt in the scheme of her life, with grocery shopping, bill balancing and keeping up with her mortgage payments, one rogue comet rated about a two on her list of important items. But she had to admit the sky was interesting.

With a weary sigh, she moved to the shelf holding the glass cage of the late Mr. Tickles. There he was, lying on his side. His mouth was open slightly and the one eye she could see was glassy, staring at nothing. She waited a second, staring at the empty eye and after a few heartbeats, she knew the poor thing was definitely dead. The still body proved it if the eye wasn't enough for her.

Sliding off the mesh cover, she reached inside and plucked the gerbil from the sawdust of the cage, wrapping the small furry body in the paper towel.

She set the small corpse on the shelf, while she covered the cage again. It was an instinctual thing, the gesture certainly not necessary.

After sliding the cover over the cage, she reached out for Mr. Tickles and was shocked to see the paper towel moving slightly, like the tiny fur ball had been sleeping and was now awake.

Scratching her head at the weird turn of events, she reached out to unwrap the paper towel, feeling uplifted she could tell her daughter Mr. Tickles was all right. Maybe he had been sleeping, but when she thought about the dead eye and immobile body, she tried to tell herself she and her daughter must have been mistaken.

With one hand on the paper towel while she unwrapped it, and the other now on the lid of the cage to slide it off again, ready to set Mr. Tickles back inside his glass home, she gasped in shock when the small fur ball was exposed for her to see him clearly.

Where there was once a small, cute furry bundle of joy, there was now a feral little monster. The teeth were flared, looking sharp for all their minuteness and the eyes seemed to glow with rage.

Michelle took all this in at a glance and her mouth was open, as she prepared to call down to her daughter, when the gerbil leaped off the shelf, straight for her gaping mouth. Before Michelle could dodge away, Mr. Tickles was in her mouth; and crawling down her throat! Her teeth snapped down instinctively, severing the gerbil's tale, the twitching appendage falling to the floor in between her feet.

She didn't notice as she was gasping for air. Mr. Tickles was clogging her windpipe, and try as she might, she felt her lungs screaming for oxygen. Turning, she tried to run out of the bedroom, knowing she was choking to death, but she made it no more than three feet before her vision grew dim and her head felt like it was going to explode. There was a mirror on the wall and she saw her face, her complexion turning blue from lack of oxygen. Her flailing hands reached up to her throat, and she could see Mr. Tickles as he made his way down her neck and into her chest. Her mouth was open again, and she tried to suck in air, like a fish out of water, but there was none for her to take in. Her head felt like mush and as she fell to the floor unconscious, her head cracked the corner of the bureau. A deep gash in her forehead opened wide, her blood seeping into the carpet as she landed heavily on the floor. She arched her back once in her final death throes, and then lay still. Her eyes took on the same glassy stare Mr. Tickles had worn only seconds ago. Her body laid still, Michelle now completely dead and if anyone had been watching, they would have figured that was the end of an innocent life.

But they would be wrong.

Five minutes passed quietly and then the side of Michelle began to move, undulate as if there was something inside her that was trying to get out. And that was exactly what was happening. Under her shirt, the flesh moved, rolled and stretched until a small set of incisors finally ripped through its meat prison. Pushing the shirt aside, the now bloody Mr. Tickles crawled out of the large gash and crawled to the floor. His fur was matted and his stomach was stretched to breaking, filled with Michelle's insides. The dead animal had gorged itself, but despite this it was still hungry, starving in fact. Already its nose was sniffing the air as it searched for fresh meat.

Footsteps sounded from down the hallway and tiny feet could be heard approaching the bedroom.

"Mommy? I got tired of waiting. I thought maybe I could help you. Is Mr. Tickles gonna be okay?"

Michelle's daughter moved to the bedroom door and stopped cold, staring down at the bloody mess of her mother.

She never saw the crimson blur jump from the floor and latch onto her face until it was far too late to do anything more than scream.

Four minutes later, both mother and daughter rose from the blood drenched carpeting and looked around with dead eyes. They were both hungry and daddy would be home from work in a few minutes.

Leaving the bedroom behind, they went into the living room to wait for him.

Saugus, Massachusetts

Little Timmy Monahan was going on seven. He was in his backyard, playing with his trucks. Every now and then his eyes would drift to the small, fresh mound of dirt a few feet away near the tall six foot fence that bordered the yard.

A tear came to his eyes and he felt his nose getting stuffy as he thought about what was under that mound of dirt.

It was his pet rabbit, named Cottontail. He had owned the rabbit for over a year and had loved the animal deeply. Then for some unknown reason, Cottontail had died. His father had buried him in a cardboard box in the backyard two months ago and had even stuck a small wooden cross he'd made in his workshop in the basement.

Now Timmy tried to ignore the small grave and play with his trucks. Overhead, the yellow sky was clear; no clouds in sight, but Timmy could have cared less about the odd looking horizon. He'd heard his dad and mom talking about the comet and that was good enough for him. Besides, if there was anything to be worried about, he knew his parents would tell him.

So filling his dump truck with pine cones and dirt, he pushed/pretend-drove the toy three feet to his left, where he had made a small construction zone with his other trucks.

While he played, he at first didn't notice the small mound of dirt begin to shift, then slowly begin to vibrate, as if something underneath was trying to return to the surface.

So Timmy played, while behind him a dirty, white and gray furred paw broke the surface of the earth, the paw scraping away at the small hole which soon grew in size. Timmy played while the rabbit named Cottontail pulled itself free of its earthly grave. Bits of plastic bag clung to its head and ears from where it had chewed its way out of the garbage bag it had been buried in. Other bits of cardboard still were protruding from its mouth, relics of tearing through the cardboard shoebox.

Timmy never knew there was something incredibly amazing and frightening happening behind him until Cottontail had fully pulled himself out of the hole and was shaking off his fur. Ants covered his furry face, crawling in and out of his ears and nose and the rabbit shook its head, trying to dislodge most of them.

The sound of the rabbit dislodging the ants from its body was subtle, like a soft sneeze, but it was enough to make Timmy turn around. His eyes lit up with both shock and happiness upon seeing Cottontail standing over the grave.

"Cottontail! You're alive! I knew dad was wrong about you!" Timmy yelled.

Spinning on his knees, Timmy moved closer and reached out to pick up his beloved pet, small hands wrapping around the dirt-covered body. Timmy held Cottontail up to his face and at first he didn't notice the foul smelling odor of death. But then his eyes went wider and he scrunched his nose up, realizing something was wrong here. He saw the ants and a few maggots fall out of the rabbit's nose and he opened his mouth in terror.

And that was when Cottontail kicked off his arms, hind legs pressing off Timmy's wrists, the small animal lunging for Timmy's throat. The small boy fell back, startled, and before he could do anything to protect himself, sharp teeth sunk into his tender neck, blood shooting out to cover the rabbit in crimson. Timmy's arms fell to his side and he began to spasm, his carotid artery severed by those sharp teeth. Legs kicked out and the rabbit dove deeper, soon its head disappearing into the neck wound like it was burrowing into a hole in the ground.

Timmy stopped moving and the dead rabbit continued feeding.

Six and a half minutes later, Timmy's mother looked out the kitchen window to see her baby lying in the dirt. Dropping the lettuce she was washing for dinner, she ran out the back door, forgetting the pot of water boiling for pasta.

When she reached her boy, she grabbed the meat engorged rabbit, tossed it away and reached down, cradling Timmy's still body in her arms.

"Timmy! Timmy, oh God, no! Wake up, honey. It's Mommy!"

And then Timmy did wake up. His eyes snapped open and his mouth went wide, and though he still had almost all his baby teeth, the small jaw sunk into his mother's jugular, chewing heartily, gnawing like he was a starving Ethiopian given a banquet of chicken and rice. Timmy's mother managed one scream and not being able to push her baby away from her, her motherly instincts overwhelming her own sense of survival, she cradled her undead son in her arms, while she passed out from blood loss.

Seven and a half minutes later, mom revived, and with her son next to her, the two exited the backyard and onto the street, already searching for more human meat. Behind the two shambling forms, a now fat bunny followed them, hopping happily with teeth bared for all to see.

Las Vegas, Nevada

The sun beat down on George Frinkle's head, causing him to perspire more profusely. Wiping his brow with a handkerchief, he stared at the yellow hued horizon, all thanks to the comet, and then he gazed down at the dead cat lying at his feet.

It was Winky, the family cat, and had been for over thirteen years.

Unfortunately, Winky had gone to sleep last night and had never woken up. George had taken the dead animal from his pet bed in the back room, and with his wife crying tears of loss, had wrapped the cat in a plastic bag and carried the carcass out to the backyard.

Which brings him to the here and now.

Picking up the shovel from the yellow and wilted grass, thanks to yet another water rationing, and why would anyone want to build a city in the middle of the desert, anyway, he began digging a hole in the ground. This would be Winky's final resting place till the end of time.

George wasn't an active man and after the fourth shovelful of dirt he was breathing harder. Slowing his digging, he paused for yet another moment, hoping something would happen to let him put off the physical exertion of burying the dead cat.

He got his wish, but not the way he might have expected.

To his mild surprise, the plastic bag began to move! And the sound of Winky mewling and growling came to his ears. For the first ten seconds he was stunned and dropped the shovel to the grass. He looked back to the house, wanting to call out to his wife, tell her Winky wasn't dead after all, but she was nowhere to be seen.

Then the cat began to cry and his attention was focused on the white, kitchen trash bag again.

The bag was shifting, the top of the bag bouncing up and down as Winky tried to escape his prison. Fearing for the cat's life, not wanting the animal to suffocate, George dropped to the grass, heedless of getting his pants stained, and began ripping open the plastic bag.

As he ripped, the sound of the cat grew in pitch and his heart began beating faster as adrenalin pumped through his system.

Wow, what a story to tell the guys at the bar later tonight. It was just like in one of those old movies when they bury the person alive, only to find out they were unconscious with some illness and woke up later to fight their way from the grave, he thought.

Upon finally tearing the plastic bag from the cat's body, George's mouth dropped open when he saw the condition of the cat, plus the odor.

This animal wasn't alive, that was for sure. The sweet smell of rotting meat and bile filled his sinuses. The cat hissed and bared its fangs and George fell backward, his butt landing on the grass. He was so frazzled; he didn't have time to think about what the grass was doing to the back of his pants, the grass working itself into the material.

Sitting on the ground, he was defenseless when Winky rolled out of the bag and lunged for his throat. George let out a squeak of shock and then felt a sharp pain in his throat, right where his jugular was located. Winky tossed his head back and forth, digging deep into his neck, the blood bathing the cat's fur in crimson. George's arms were out to his side and he reached up, wanting to grab the cat and rip it from him, but no sooner did he raise his arms, then he felt lightheaded. His chest was wet with blood and for the first few seconds it was warm, but even in the warm Las Vegas day the plasma cooled quickly.

His arms dropped to their sides, and Winky continued eating, feasting in the warm flesh of George's neck.

As for George, he had already passed into that good night, and with his body lying in the sun, his wife arrived at the back door to see how he was doing burying the cat.

She screamed once, long and loud and took three faltering steps towards his supine body.

"Winky, is that you? But how?" She stuttered, barely recognizing the beloved family cat now bathed in red gore. The scarlet face shifted to look up at her and the teeth flared once more. Then, like a small leopard, the revived animal shot across the lawn and at the last moment jumped at the woman, teeth sinking into the side of her neck. She flailed and screamed, but the ferocity of the dead animal was triple-fold compared to when it was alive.

Before she could comprehend what was happening, the cat's head had disappeared inside her neck and upper chest, claws slashing her flesh to ribbons, her blood geysering in all directions. She took a few awkward steps backward on weak legs and then collapsed to the grass, her blood staining the yellow and faded-green lawn red.

While her body twitched in its final death throes, Winky continued to feed under an amber sky.

Eight minutes later, George stumbled over to his prone wife and gazed down on her still form. George's chest and arms were covered with gore and his legs swayed back and forth, barley able to hold him up. He waited for only a few minutes, when suddenly, his wife's eyes snapped open, the cat climbing off her animated corpse. She looked left and then right, and with a heave of her mangled body, climbed to her feet, her neck so ravaged by teeth she could barely support her head. With her head lolling to the right like a sagging balloon, the couple moved out of the yard and into the street, their eyes already searching for something to kill. On the ground, trotting like a good pet was Winky, his tail in the air and his dead eyes looking left and right, the family together again, even if it was only in death.

Helena, Montana

Michael Carter walked across the windswept field, gazing up at the yellow sky.

He had read about the comet in the newspaper and had been hearing about it for more than a week as the news was focusing on the event twenty-four/seven.

Not that he could blame them much. It wasn't like there was much else to do around these parts.

He paused on the ridge and took his cowboy hat off, wiping his brow with his shirtsleeve. It wasn't that warm out, but the clear sky still sent the sun's rays onto him, baking him from the outside in.

Now that he was on the ridge, he was able to see across most of his farm and grazing land and he frowned at a slumped form about two hundred feet away.

Cursing himself for not taking one of the horses from the stable, he continued onward, his destination now the shape lying in the foot-high grass.

As he moved closer, he could see the definite form of one of his cows come into focus. Oh yeah, this was the one that went missing two days ago.

By the time he was only twenty feet away from the cow, he was sweating again and he muttered curses for his own stupidity.

If he had only taken one of the horses. But he'd told his wife he needed the exercise, the fool he was for thinking that. With a weary sigh, he crossed the remaining distance to the prone animal, and when he was only fifty feet away, the wind blowing towards him, he got the first whiff of death emanating off the dead carcass.

Not a stranger to the redolence of death, he moved closer, only slightly creasing his eyes and now breathing through his mouth to try to take the bite out of the odor.

When he was only a few yards away, he frowned deeply, seeing how bad the damage was to one of his prize heifers.

The cow was covered in ants and flies, maggots squirming in the large hole in the carcass' side as they fed on the meat. He had no way of knowing how the animal had died, but he could only assume it was from one of a dozen illnesses that plagued his animals on a daily basis. Moving so he was only three feet away, he covered his nose with his right sleeve and bent over to get a better look at the dead animal. The entire side of the cow was torn open, and it was obvious scavengers had gotten to the carcass. Wolves and coyotes flourished in the nearby forest and he was only mildly surprised there wasn't more damage to the heifer.

The cow's eyes were still open, glazed and staring at nothing. Ants crawled over the eyes, seeking to partake of the soft ocular orbs, and maggots were feeding in the sockets, wiggling in happiness; or so he would imagine.

Kneeling on the grass, he counted the amount of dollars he'd just lost because this stupid animal had up and died on him. With a shake of his head, he prepared to get up and leave, planning on returning later with the backhoe. From there he would scoop the carcass up and bring it back to the main farmhouse where he would bury it on the South 40.

So caught up in his plans for how to dispose of the carcass, he never noticed when the eyelids seemed to twitch and the jaw moved a fraction of an inch on the dead face.

Waving the flies that were trying to feed on him away from his face, Michael stood up, turned and was about to walk away when he felt a sudden pain in his left calf. He screamed in pain and went down to one knee, looking down at his foot to see what had a hold of him. Images of a coyote who had skulked out of the edge of the woods came to mind, but when he saw where his leg was, he shook his head and screamed yet again.

"No, that's impossible! You're dead!" He screamed as he stared in horrified shock at the heifer as it bit deeper into his calf, the teeth grating on bone. He shrieked again and tried to escape, but the dead cow's jaw was like a bear trap.

The only way he would be releasing his leg was by cutting it off or by somehow prying open the cow's mouth.

Falling to the grass, Michael screamed and tried to pull his leg free of the cow's mouth, but all he got for his trouble was a pang of agony as strong teeth cut into his flesh.

With his other leg free, he began kicking the cow in the face, but all that did was dislodge more maggots from the eye sockets and from inside the nasal cavity.

He could only watch in horror as the cow rolled over, and on unsteady legs, actually stood up.

When the head rose, so did Michael's leg and soon he found himself almost upside down, his leg still dangling like a piece of cud. The cow pressed harder and Michael shrieked, almost passing out in pain.

Even in his despair, he tried to keep a level head, and he reached to his hip for his eight inch Bowie knife.

With shaking hands, he steadied himself on the grass, and reached up with his right hand and pulled the blade from its sheath. The cow mooed, the sound distorted thanks to his leg in its mouth and Michael was able to look over his shoulder and see the half eaten side of the cow. Organs spilled and slid out of the cavity to splash on the sodden grass and he felt his stomach preparing to let go. Almost upside down, he felt it would only come out easier when he did vomit, but even with the taste of bile in his throat, he forced it back down. There was no time for that right now. If he wanted to get free of this impossibility trying to eat him, he would need to keep a level head.

Spinning on the ground, he reached up and stabbed the cow in the left eye, all eight inches of the blade sliding home and into the cow's brain. If the dead animal noticed, it gave no indication, but merely ground down harder on his leg. Screeching in pain, he let go of the knife, the blade still embedded in the cow's eye socket.

Then the animal began shaking him around like a rag doll and he screamed in fear.

Something told him he was about to die.

The cow's jaw ground one last time and severed the bone of his leg. Michael was set free of the cow and he fell in a heap, staring up at the amber sky. He looked down at his crushed and mangled leg and his breath lodged in his chest. Where his foot used to be there was now nothing but a jagged piece of bone, looking like someone had snapped a tree branch rather sloppily, leaving a bad wound. Blood seeped from his leg and onto the grass, staining the green stalks crimson.

Already feeling lightheaded, he knew he needed to get away. First he would get away, then he would rip his shirt in half and make himself a quick tourniquet.

With the world spinning around him, he rolled onto his stomach and began crawling away. In his head, he thought he was making great time, covering vast distances, but in reality he had barely managed to cross five feet of land.

His vision grew blurry and he felt himself passing out, but not before he realized there was something blocking out the sun's rays, a shadow befalling him.

Turning his head slightly, he gazed up at the dead cow, the remaining glazed eye now more focused and staring straight down at him. He had time to let out one last scream before the cow's jaw opened impossibly wide and came down over his head. Teeth clacked shut, severing his neck and spine, and when the cow's head came back up, there was no head on Michael's shoulders. Blood seeped from the wound, but lacked any energy thanks to almost all of the fluid already leaking from the savaged leg.

Michael's headless corpse dropped to the grass and twitched a few times in death, while the cow chewed the head like a mouthful of hay.

When it was finished chewing, it swallowed, and more than half of the pulped head slipped out of the jagged hole in the side of the cow, thanks to only one of the three stomachs still being intact. Then the rest of the head went to one of the ruptured stomachs inside the dead beast, and with the taste of human meat in its mouth, the dead animal began walking away from Michael's corpse.

It mooed to the horizon, the sound hauntingly ethereal in its quality. Still a mindless beast, but a beast with a hunger for human meat, the grizzled animal began moving across the grassland, heading directly toward Michael's home...where his wife and daughter were waiting for his return, unaware of their impending fate.

Ten minutes later, give or take a few seconds, Michael's headless corpse rose from the bloodied grass. It swayed on its one remaining foot, now leaning at an awkward angle. The body swayed for a few seconds, unsure of where to go, and then like a man tossed into darkness, the body stumbled off in the opposite direction the dead cow had taken. The body tripped over roots and rocks more than once, and one time a large tree root impaled its chest, but each time the headless corpse pulled itself to its one foot and nub and headed off again.

The body continued on until reaching a small ravine, where it tumbled into a tear in the earth, where it would now be trapped for as long as its flesh held together.

If the body had still had a head with ears, it would have heard the screams of a woman and young girl, their shrieks of terror and pain floating on the wind like a nightingale's song.

Penn Valley, California

The school bell for recess rang and the children of the Kennedy Middle School charged into the playground, their young minds already on games of tag and jump rope and dodge ball.

Little Domenic Giordano crossed the hot pavement, walking away from the other children, until he was on the hardtop of the track which surrounded the football field; the boy seeking shade under the bleachers in the far corner of the school yard.

He was alone, as always.

Domenic was a loner, and had been one for his entire young life. A few other kids called to him, but he waved them away, preferring his own company.

Passing through a bunch of kids tossing a tennis ball around, he moved to the bleachers and slipped underneath.

Immediately he felt better, the metal stairs blocking the sun's rays. The sky was an odd color, but he barely gave it a second's thought. He was ten and there were far more important things to worry about other than a yellow sky, like Naruto, Star Wars and wrestling.

At first he didn't notice the small, feathered shape in the corner, near the chain link fence, and he looked at the ground around him, seeing if there was any money lying in the debris. The currency would fall from the pockets of the patrons when they came to see a football game. It was then he realized there was something under the bleachers with him.

With nothing better to do, and his curiosity peaked, he strolled to the opposite end with both hands in his pants pockets, his eyes peering through the shadows at the small creature lying on the ground. When he reached the tiny shape, he realized it was a seagull. Sometimes the birds would come to the schoolyard looking for leftovers from the football games. Usually, underneath the bleachers was a cornucopia of popcorn, bits of candy, and dropped containers of soda, some with leftover syrupy goodness still in the bottoms of the cups.

Unfortunately, there were some people who were beyond cruel and they would shove Alka-Seltzer tablets into the food and then feed it to the seagulls. This was one of those poor birds. It was obviously dead, its lower half resembling an exploded melon. Where the breast of the bird should be there was a gaping hole, a red fuzz dripping out like when a laundry machine has had too much detergent placed inside it while doing a load of laundry. The head was still, and Domenic knew the bird was definitely dead. With nothing else to do, he picked up a stick near his foot and began poking the dead bird. This kept him occupied for only a few minutes, and when he began to get bored and was about to leave, his eyes spotted a shiny dime just on the other side of the seagull's beak.

Dropping the stick, he leaned over to fetch the coin, already thinking about how he would add it to his collection at home, when suddenly the seagull's beak snapped up and bit deep into his wrist, severing his radial artery with its sharp point.

It happened so fast Domenic at first didn't realize what had happened. The beak slicing into his flesh seemed like only a sting at first, but then his nerves woke up and his brain was sent the unbelievable agony as the beak bit deep and ripped a small gobbet of flesh from his arm. His blood sprayed across the underside of the bleachers and he cried out. Turning to run away, he was stopped in his tracks when he saw more than a dozen field mice, and a few rats thrown in for good measure, lining up behind him. Their whiskers flicked and tails snapped back and forth, and even in his pain, Domenic could see these rodents weren't healthy. Hell, some of them appeared to be downright dead. A few seemed to pulse as the maggots within continued to feed, ignoring the fact their meal was on the move and mobile.

With his free hand covering his wound, and blood squirting through his fingers, Domenic backed away from the rodents. Unfortunately, he tripped over the seagull which was trying to right itself, its beak now stained crimson from his blood. He fell heavily to the dirt and cried out, but with all the kids playing across the field, there was no one to hear him.

The rodents swarmed over him, each open mouth biting and tearing. The seagull managed to crawl to his face, and with beak closed tightly, the head darted forward, plucking the boy's right eye out like it was a piece of food floating in the ocean. The seagull opened its mouth and scooped the tidbit into its maw, then went back for more.

Domenic rolled around on the ground, and when he tried to scream again, his mouth was filled with the decayed carcass of a dead rat, the creature sliding down his throat as it ate its way into his body.

With the children of the middle school running and playing only a hundred feet away, Domenic was eaten alive, until he, too, died, joining the dead animals devouring him whole.

When he revived, his ears immediately picked up the sounds of laughter and playing. Climbing to his feet, he headed out of the bleachers, the horde of rats and other rodents by his side, the playing children about to receive an unexpected surprise.

Minutes later, the sounds of laughter turned to sounds of pain and fright, Timmy relishing his newfound power.

He wasn't alone anymore.

Now, he had friends, lots of them, and all were dead like him.

New York City

Martin Sota and Vinnie Ferrara walked down 22nd street, a hotdog in each of their right hands, chewing happily. The two were off for the day, wanting to catch the baseball game. Both had called in sick, saying they were coming down with a cold.

It didn't matter if their boss believed them, the two had sick days saved and those days were theirs to take. Sure they shouldn't use them for seeing a baseball game, but what was the fun of taking a sick day when you were sick?

The sky was overcast, the amber sky an odd picture over the New York skyline, the horizon peeking through the high-rises. Both men moved with fluidity through the busy sidewalk, dodging pedestrians like the local New Yorkers they were. Born and raised in the city and damn proud of it.

A male pedestrian bumped Vinnie and he spun, aggravated. "Hey, you jerk, I'm walkin' here!"

The pedestrian never so much as turned around and Vinnie flipped the guy off, then continued onward; Martin barely slowing for his friend.

"So, Vinnie," Martin said, chomping on his hotdog, "you see that zombie flick at the multiplex yet?"

"What, you mean the one with the kids in the Winnebago? Nah, not yet. Probably won't either. I mean come on, give me a good slasher flick any day, but zombies? Please, how unreal can you get?"

Martin frowned, a die hard fan since he was a kid.

"What, you don't think zombies are real? What about all that shit in Haiti and Louisiana. Zombies are real enough, my friend."

Vinnie made a raspberry and took a bite of his hotdog, the topping falling off to slop onto the sidewalk, leaving a mess for his fellow pedestrians. "Please, zombies are about as real as ghosts."

Martin's eyebrows went up in a challenge.

"Oh yeah? Now you're saying you don't believe in ghosts? Well, listen to this then, here's why ghosts and zombies are real and why they're not just imagination." He popped the last morsel of his hotdog into his mouth, preparing to give his speech.

He held up his hand, still covered in mustard from his finished hotdog and prepared to begin counting off why zombies and ghosts were not figments of the imagination when sounds of screaming and honking horns could be heard coming from up the street. Now normally this wouldn't be such a big deal in the Big Apple, but these noises sounded off, more intense, the screaming filled with terror instead of just anger.

"What the fuck is going on up there; an accident?" Vinnie asked, trying to see over the heads of the other pedestrians.

Martin lowered his hand, wiping it absently on his trousers. "Don't know, maybe." He strained to see, too, but there were far too many people. It was a little after twelve p.m. and the street was packed as always.

Then a thunderous crash sounded and a large gray cloud blocked out the amber sky.

"What the fuck is that?" Vinnie asked, shielding his eyes to get a better view. All around him people were stopping, some curious, but more than half barely acknowledging what was happening, too absorbed in their daily lives to care.

"Don't know, a cloud? But it's moving awful fast for a cloud and it's so low to the ground," Martin said, his curiosity peaked.

Then came the sounds of flapping wings and screams and the echo of hundreds of footsteps on the sidewalk and pavement. Cars screeched to a halt, more horns sounded and the shattering of glass and the crunch of metal filled the air.

Then both Martin and Vinnie saw what the so called cloud really was.

Thousands of pigeons, all festering and rotting, were flying down from the surrounding buildings. These thousands of the birds once lined the edges of buildings and rooftops across the city, their dead carcasses merely an annoyance to the maintenance personnel all over the city. Parks were full of the small, feathered bodies, hidden in bushes and shrubs across Central Park and beyond. The dead birds were a part of the city, like the rubbish and the congested traffic. No one gave them much notice…at least until they rose from the dead to attack the living.

Martin and Vinnie were caught in an onrush of humanity and people tried to escape the attacking flock. Before either man could stop themselves, they were forced to the street as hundreds of feet stepped on them. Martin cried out when a heavy boot crushed his left index finger, breaking the digit in half. Vinnie received a boot to the face and the man screamed imprecations at the crowd flowing over him. Reaching out, he grabbed for legs and arms, trying to pull himself to his feet. By luck alone, the two men managed to crawl to the edge of the sidewalk and out of the worst of the running New Yorkers. They thought they were safe, but then they realized their ordeal was only beginning.

The reason why the New Yorkers were running was the murderous flock of birds now descending on the racing pedestrians. Beaks dove for eyes and claws raked necks and cheeks, causing more chaos in the street. Both Martin and Vinnie looked up and had enough time to raise their hands in defense before a score of birds covered them, beaks pecking out their eyes and tearing open their throats. But they weren't alone, as all around them their fellow New Yorkers were being slaughtered by the hundreds. Then, as if things couldn't get any worse, from out of the sewers flowed rats, thousands of them, all bloated and maggot infested from decomposing in the city sewers for years. Some were nothing but slime and bones, the slick rodents nipping at the hells of the running pedestrians. A woman went down and she tried to shield her five-year-old daughter, but in seconds both were overwhelmed, a hundred times two of fangs and teeth biting out one inch chunks of their flesh. Like piranhas of the earth, the rats gorged themselves on the tidbits, while the pigeons dived bombed their prey from the sky. A few birds managed to get inside cabs, their wings flapping as they pecked out eyes, the humans trapped inside the metal and glass boxes on wheels. Both Martin and Vinnie were enveloped, their bodies picked clean from the inside out, leaving nothing but a few tufts of clothing and the chewed on bones.

All across New York, the same carnage was happening, and soon explosions rocked the city as multiple accidents and crashes compounded the terror. A gas truck ran a red-light, the driver fighting off a dozen pigeons who had flown into his cab. He jumped the curb and plowed into a Starbucks, taking out everyone hiding within, the tank of fuel igniting in a blazing fireball. The smell of fresh roasted coffee beans filled the street, along with another aroma, an odor that was sickly sweet and was reminiscent of fire roasted pig. The conflagration quickly spread, with other buildings joining, and soon the north side of town was a roaring inferno, any humans trapped within dead or dying.

And still the undead animals attacked, devouring all who were in sight.

But it was only later that things truly grew unimaginable, as each fresh corpse, each mangled and devoured cadaver, rose from the streets and began to wander away.

And now, they too, were in search of fresh meat…human meat.

New York was soon to become a city of the dead, and God help any who remained within its city limits.

Eagan, Michigan

Joe Franks walked down the four foot hallway towards the walk-in freezer at the end of the drab hall. In his hands was a three foot black plastic bag.

Inside the bag, the plastic stretching against the object within, could be seen the outline of a canine face.

The animal was very dead; euthanized only five minutes ago.

Joe felt little for the animal. He had learned quickly in his new job as a euthanizer at the Eagan County Animal Shelter that if he let his emotions rule his actions; he would never sleep a wink at night. For all purposes, he was an executioner, putting good, lovable animals to death simply because no one wanted them. But someone had to do it and it might as well be him. After all, the pay wasn't bad and the hours were great.

There were times when he hated his job, of course, but for now he was all right with it. The dog in his arms was an old one, and by putting the animal to sleep, he had saved it endless suffering.

Upon reaching the walk-in freezer, he opened the door and stepped inside, his breath clouding in front of his face. He dropped the bag casually on the four foot pile of bags already within, telling himself he would need to call for a pickup soon. The carcasses would be brought to a local funeral home where they would be cremated, the funeral director making some money on the side.

After dropping the bag down, Joe reached into his shirt pocket and pulled out a pack of Marlboros. The freezer was a great place to smoke, as it was a self contained environment. As long as he didn't mind freezing his balls off, he was able to get in a quick break with no one the wiser.

Turning his back on the pile of dog and cat corpses, he lit his cigarette and sucked in deeply, feeling that invigorating rush when the smoke filled his lungs.

Joe didn't watch that much television and had heard nothing about the comet, and wouldn't have cared if he had.

While he leaned against the door jamb and puffed away, behind him the plastic bags began to rustle and shift. Joe was oblivious, the motor of the freezer chugging away, hiding any sound the plastic bags may have made.

While Joe smoked and thought of his upcoming date with a slutty chick he had picked up at a local bar last week, the bags shifted and began to tear behind him. Canine teeth chewed through the bags and feline claws sliced like small razors.

In less than two minutes, half the bags insides were exposed, the carcasses of the frozen animals slowly moving. They would have moved faster, but the freezer had severely hampered their limbs, but whatever had reanimated them was able to overcome the freezing temperatures, and one at a time the animals crawled out of the pile, with more freeing themselves of their plastic bag prisons with each passing second.

Joe finished his cigarette and dropped it onto the floor. Stepping on it, he prepared to pick it up, planning on shoving it into one of the animal bags, thereby hiding the evidence.

His jaw fell open and his voice lodged in his throat when he saw the line of animals moving towards him.

He managed a squeak of a scream before the first dog was on him. The Pit-bull was a fierce animal in life, having bitten three people before being put down, and it was even fiercer in death. Joe raised his hands in defense and the Pit-bull sank its incisors into his arm, the razor sharp teeth closing on bone.

Now Joe screamed loudly, but with the freezer door closed, no one could hear him. Ten cats, all of different sizes and colors, swarmed around his legs, scratching deep grooves through his pants and into his skin. Blood seeped into his sneakers and his legs felt numb as his warm blood turned ice cold in the below-zero freezer. A small Doberman pincher came at him and he punched it in the face with his free arm. His fist connected with the animal's left eye and the frozen orb shattered under the blow, but the animal still had another and quickly latched onto his wrist with its teeth. With arms trapped between the two animals, Joe was brought to the floor. It was only when another set of canine teeth sank into his neck that he realized he was about to die.

Pushing the Pit-bull off him, and losing a four inch chunk of his arm for his trouble, he reached up and unlocked the freezer latch. Then the teeth around his neck squeezed harder and his spine snapped; his jugular pierced from the pressure at the same time.

As Joe fell into the cold embrace of death, he wondered if this was some sort of poetic justice. That the god of animals everywhere had finally come to Earth to seek vengeance on him for all the animals he had killed. Then he lost consciousness and slid into the eternity of death, the reanimated animals still feeding on his corpse.

Eight minutes and twenty nine seconds later, Joe stirred on the ground. His face was a jagged mess of torn flesh and gristle and only one eye still worked. His torso was chewed to the point there was nothing left, and the few remaining organs spilled out to slop onto the ground, freezing to the floor in seconds.

The freezer door was still ajar and he pushed it open some more, the animals following him down the hallway.

On wobbly legs, Joe hobbled down the hallway, a crimson streak trailing behind him while he began to thaw out, and upon reaching the entrance to the main room of the animal shelter, he stepped into the waiting room with the army of dead animals behind him.

Everyone in the waiting room looked up at the same time, mouths agape at the sight of the dead man and his minions. With one gnawed and torn arm, Joe raised it into the air, and when he dropped it, the dead cats and dogs swarmed into the room, teeth flaring and claws out, attacking everyone in sight.

The screams went on for much longer than anyone would have thought possible. That is, if anyone had been alive to hear them.

New Hampshire, 20 miles south of Portsmouth

Michael Carver strolled through the woods, his hiking boots crunching under the soft sod overlaid with leaves and twigs. The odor of pine filled his sinuses and the sun peeked through the treetops overhead, the odd amber color unsettling.

Still, he had decided to go hiking today, and he'd be damned if he would cancel because the sky looked weird. His cell phone was in his front pocket and he pulled it out, wanting to check for messages. It was a habit, and the instant he checked, he saw there was no signal.

Of course not, you idiot, you're in the middle of the woods, for Christ sakes, he thought.

Shoving the phone back into his pocket, he slowed near a few prone logs. The mighty logs had once been trees of more than a hundred years old, but a bad storm had taken them down. Now the bark was flaking off like a human arm with an advanced case of leprosy.

Dropping down onto one of the logs, he pulled out his I-pod, placed the earpieces in his ears and cranked up some Aerosmith. He was an old school rocker and his friends didn't understand his taste in music at all. Fresh from college, he had a taste for nostalgia, right down to the 1969 Camaro he had parked back at the beginning of the path.

Drinking heavily from a bottle of water, he wiped his mouth on his sleeve and stood up. Feeling better now that he wasn't as parched, he began moving out again. He had at least three more miles to cover before he would loop around and head back to his car. With a shifting of his backpack, he took his first step forward and promptly stopped in mid-stride, his leg hovering in the air.

There was a large Black bear in front of him and that would be something to fear on any day of the year, but what was truly unsettling was the condition of the animal. It was missing its right, front paw. Unknown to Michael, the bear had been caught in a poacher's snare and the bear trap had snapped shut on the animal's leg. The bear had managed to pull itself free, but only after literally tearing its paw off. Then the poor animal had bled out, dropping to the forest floor to die.

But now it was back, and with three other legs to carry it forward. It had been on the prowl for hours, looking for food, namely human.

And Michael fit the bill perfectly.

Shaking his head as he stared at the large beast, unable to believe his bad luck, Michael began backing away, hoping he could outdistance the wounded animal and make for a tree. He figured if he climbed up high enough he could stay safe. Of course he didn't know what he would do then, but one thing at a time.

Ever so slowly, he tried to back up, one leg at a time, careful not to trip on hidden obstacles. Just as he the cleared logs, he spun, preparing to run for all he was worth. He didn't go three yards before he was stopped yet again.

There were two wolves in front of him, both looking haggard and worn out. Their ribcage poked through their fur, and it was apparent the two animals were starving to death, or had starved to death. With heads low to the ground, the wolves snarled, and Michael looked for a way out of his predicament, but unfortunately he didn't see one.

Pulling a small hunting knife from his waist, the blade no more than six inches long, he felt woefully under armed.

"Okay, you bastards. Let's dance," he said, his voice squeaking, belaying his attempt at bravado. The two wolves prepared to launch themselves at the man, but before they could, there was a crashing of the brush behind him and the Black bear was on him.

He had been so focused on the new threat he had forgotten the bear!

He spun to face the new threat and claws raked his chest, tearing his clothing to shreds. He screamed; his body filled with fire. It was like there was acid in his veins!

His torso felt warm and then cold and he looked down to see red squirting out of a jagged chest wound. He could see the white of his ribs peeking through the tear in his flesh and he opened his mouth to scream yet again. But before he could, the two wolves attacked him, going for his legs. One sank teeth into his right calf, the other his left shin, both shaking their heads back and forth as they worried at the appendages. He was thrown to the ground and he smelled pine needles again, only this time he smelled something else along side it.

His own death as his bowels let go.

With Aerosmith screaming in his ears, his own shrieks of death filled the forest wall. The reanimated animals were hungry and there would be nothing left of the man to return when they were through with the human food.

When the bear and wolves were through, other animals appeared, all in some form of decay. Mice, squirrels, a few carrion birds, and a set of chipmunks all attacked the body, feeding on whatever remained. Despite there being shattered bones and severed limbs, a bloodied finger of the corpse twitched in the moist soil. Even in this state of visceral carnage and disrepair, the undead flesh tried to reanimate. Despite there not being enough of the body to move this prone form of bile and torn meat, the creature who was once Michael Carver would try anyway, while nearby, lying on the ground, the I-pod continued to play.

At least until the battery ran out.

3

TROUBLE ON THE HIGHWAY

"**W**HAT'S WRONG, THERE, Sweety Pie, you don't look happy?" Pastor Martin James asked Beth while they drove down the highway.

Overhead, the yellow sky seemed to pulse and flow with a mind of its own, resembling an ocean.

Beth had been in the car for a little more than a half hour and she already knew Pastor James was a man of the cloth in name only. Even now, while he asked her how she was, his right hand was sliding across the seat to touch her thigh. This wasn't the first time either. Since pulling off the shoulder of the road, he had constantly tried to touch her, sometimes with casual tricks and other times with flat out reaching. He was a horndog, pure and simple.

Beth was concentrating on the radio, moving the dial back and forth as she tried to pull in a signal. With the White Mountains and other, smaller ones all around her, reception could sometimes become spotty.

Finally she settled on a station, though the voice was fading in and out.

"There seems to be reports of unusual disturbances coming from all across the wire," the announcer said. "Reports of animal attacks are coming in with more and more frequency. Some of these reports are a little bizarre. We are getting details that some of the animals appear to be dead." The announcer chuckled then. "Now, I know how that sounds, folks, and of course we here at KBBO will be looking into it further, but for now there is one thing everyone should do. Stay off the streets and remain in your homes or workplaces. Wait until the authorities can work out whatever is happening. We'll be covering this story for as long as it…" The voice faded away and static filled the car speakers. Frowning, Beth tried to get the announcer back, but it was hopeless.

"Give it up, Sweety Pie; you know how bad reception is in these mountains." His hand was crawling up her thigh again and he managed to reach the inner part of her leg. Slowly, with his eyes on the road, he began sliding his hand towards the junction of her thighs.

Beth stopped fiddling with the radio and turned her head to stare at him.

"Look, *Pastor*, if you don't get your hand off my leg right now, the next time you try to jerk off you can do it with a stump."

The hand was snatched back and Pastor James' mouth dropped open.

"Oh my, what a mouth on you. Back in my day, a lady would never speak to a man of the cloth like that."

Beth sneered, "Yeah, well, sorry to tell you, but this is my day now, and I'm telling you to keep your hands off me."

Pastor James tried to look as flustered as he could manage given the circumstances and he turned to look at her, taking his eyes off the road, when Beth screamed for him to look out. Pastor James turned to look out the windshield, but he was too late.

A stray dog had wandered onto the highway and before Pastor James could stop, he struck the animal head on, the front bumper hitting and then propelling the animal twenty feet into the air. The dog spun in the air like it was shot from a cannon and then dropped to the pavement, to roll three times before stopping. Pastor James hit the brakes and the Cadillac screeched across the highway, turning sideways in a pall of burned rubber.

Inside the car, both passengers were white as sheets and over a minute passed before Beth spoke up.

"Oh shit, you hit a dog," she gasped, gazing at the still form of the animal fifteen feet in front of the car.

"It's not my fault, I swear, the damn thing came out of nowhere. You saw it, right? I had no chance."

She didn't answer, but instead opened the passenger door and stepped out onto the highway. On the other side of the road, a few cars and a truck drove by, but none were interested in what was happening on the opposite side of the strip of green grass separating the north and south sides of the highway.

"W…w…wait, where are you going?" Pastor James asked in a stuttering voice. He was still pretty shook up from the collision.

Beth stopped and leaned over, looking back into the car.

"I'm gonna see if that dog is still alive. A real man would do it for me, but seems there's just you…" She left the rest hanging.

Pastor James sat taller in his seat and then opened his door, stepping out into the light of the day.

"Now, you just hold on there, missy. I'm as much a man as the next fella. You just sit back down and I'll see what's going on here with that dog. Hell, its got to be dead after that. Did you see the way it flew off my bumper?" He walked to the front of his car and began yelling a blue streak. "Oh, hell, would you look at that? Stupid dog dented my bumper." He leaned closer. "And some of my grille is broken. Do you know how much that'll cost to fix? That ain't covered under my insurance, ya know."

Beth looked at him with indifference and pointed to the prone dog on the highway.

"Just go, ya big baby," she prodded.

With another look at his grille and bumper, Pastor James moved off. Deep down inside himself, he hoped if he did what she wanted, he still might get lucky later.

While he walked, he gazed up at the amber sky.

Damn, sure was weird, all yellowy like that, he thought.

But he wasn't interested in comets, planets or stars. No, the good Lord was all he needed…and a quickie every now and then on the side never hurt either. After all, it said right in the good book to breed and be merry, or so he interpreted it like that.

Upon reaching the last two yards from the animal he slowed, his eyes trying to take in everything at once. There was a spreading pool of blood on the hardtop and flies were already gathering, sipping at the syrupy goodness. He idly wondered how the flies always found blood and dead things so fast. Was there some kind of alarm that rang like in a firehouse? The alarm telling the flies that dinner was served somewhere nearby.

Shaking his head at the ridiculous thoughts, he moved closer to the animal. It looked like a German shepherd, though with all the blood and gore covering the brown coat it was hard to tell. The lower cavity of the body was a shattered mess of entrails and internal organs and it was pretty obvious the animal was as dead as a living creature could get.

Despite this, he leaned down to check for a pulse, grimacing as he touched the blood-soaked fur near the neck. He tried for over a minute and then gave up.

Oh yes, this dog was definitely dead.

"Well, is he okay?" Beth called from the car, leaning against the right quarter panel.

He wanted to yell at her, tell her to get off his car before she scratched it with her belt buckle or something, when the dog's head lifted from the pavement.

Pastor James never saw the movement, too caught up with watching Beth, and no sooner did he look back then the open jaws of the dog snapped at him, sharp teeth sinking into his left wrist.

He shrieked in pain and fright, not understanding what was happening. Pulling away from the dog, the teeth held firm and he found himself dragging the animal with him. The spine of the dog was pulverized and it could do nothing from the neck down, but the jaws worked fine and they now attempted to cut his arm in half.

Bent at an odd angle, he began trying to reach the car, yelling for help. The dog sawed at his wrist, its intestines and bile spilling out of the gaping wound on its body. James looked down at the animal and his breath lodged in his throat when both predator and prey made eye contact.

Pastor James had known evil in his life, but what he saw in those undead eyes chilled him to the bone.

Then the dog's teeth sunk deeper, grating on bone and he screamed high and loud.

His shirt was covered in sweat and tears ran down his cheeks as he tried to free himself from this hellhound from Lucifer's den. His heart was beating so fast he wondered if he might have a heart attack and his vision was growing dim from the shock of the bite when suddenly he heard the roar of an eight cylinder engine. *His* eight cylinder engine to be exact.

Before he knew what was happening, a red blur was coming at him. He raised his right hand in front of him, as if that could somehow prevent him from becoming the new hood ornament on his shiny red Cadillac, when at the last instant, the car swerved around him, the left front tire missing him by an inch, but not the limp carcass of the dog. One second teeth were securely fastened to his wrist, and the next he was free, the dog becoming caught in the wheel well of the car as the body was churned inside like it had fallen into a blender.

There was one yelp from the dog and then there was nothing but the sound of wet meat and pieces of dog striking the warm pavement. The car shot past Pastor James, spraying him with blood and gore like it was wet slush on a snowy day, and after moving a hundred feet down the road, the brakes were locked and the car squealed to a halt. Pastor James stood motionless, staring at the brake lights of his car. Then the reverse lights flashed on and the car began backing up. When the rear bumper was a foot from his legs, the vehicle stopped, and Beth hopped out of the driver's seat.

She stared at Pastor James, now covered in gobbets of meat and blood from the churned up dog and she shook her head. Moving towards him, she carefully led him back to the car, opening the passenger door so he could sit down. Pastor James was still in shock, and he did what he was told, blood dripping from his jagged wrist wound. He never said a word when he sat in the car, not worrying about getting blood on his leather seats.

Beth climbed inside and closed the door, moving around the steering wheel. She ripped a small piece of her shirt off herself and quickly bandaged his wrist, talking to him the entire time.

Pastor James said nothing, his eyes glazed. But then Beth leaned forward to help him more and he was able to look down her shirt. His eyes went from staring forward to slowly turning downward, his view now of a pair of perfect, but small breasts peeking up through her loose shirt. She wore no bra.

Beth stopped talking and after a second, Pastor James slowly pulled his eyes away from those sweet mounds of flesh and looked up at her face. She was staring at him and he realized he'd just been caught peeking down her shirt. He smiled slightly, trying to look innocent.

She returned the smile, and before he could stop her, she yanked hard on the bandage, cinching the ends tighter than necessary, causing him to yelp out in pain.

"Pervert," she said slightly annoyed. "I try to help you and you try to sneak a peek at my goodies. You're one hell of a Pastor, you know that?"

He merely shrugged. He had nothing to say, which was a rarity. He felt like a child getting caught sneaking a cookie before dinner.

"Sorry?" He asked and suggested at the same time.

Disgusted, Beth moved back behind the wheel and put the car in drive. Making sure it was clear, she drove away, a trail of bloody tire prints left behind to mar the pavement. Flies were already gathering around the carcass of the dog, feasting on the gory meal.

Beth gazed in the rearview mirror and then looked forward, concentrating on the road ahead. Her eyes flicked askance of her to see Pastor James hugging his wounded arm.

"You okay?"

"No, I'm not okay. What kind of a question is that? That foul beast tried to eat me. I don't understand it. That animal sure looked dead, the good Lord as my witness."

"Maybe it wasn't, I mean, you just thought it was. Sometimes in the war my dad said men would get gut shot and live for days. That could have been what happened." Even as she said this, she didn't really believe it. The radio announcer's words came back to her and she tried to push them down. Strange occurrences. Attacks by animals. Could it be related to the dog?

Pastor James was talking and she turned her head. "What did you say?"

"I said I owe you a debt of gratitude, there, Sweety Pie. That was quick thinking on your part, though you did get my car covered in blood. Do you know how hard it is going to be to get out all that fur and blood out of the cracks in the wheel wells?"

Beth sneered at him, not caring in the least. "Sorry, Pastor, next time I'll let the dog eat you, how 'bout that?"

He looked down at the floorboards and then cradled his arm some more, wincing with the movement. The bandage was already dark with blood and Beth frowned at the sight.

"We need to get you to a hospital or somewhere where you can get that looked at," she told him.

"Fine with me, but I don't have any insurance. Cost too much. We need to go where they'll look at it for free. Like a clinic or something."

"Well, don't look at me; I don't know where to go. I'm just passing through, remember?"

Pastor James nodded, the gesture causing him pain. "Well, so am I, Sweety Pie."

Beth shook her head, changing the subject. "That dog had to be dead. It just had to be. I mean, what else could there be if that wasn't the truth?"

Pastor James didn't answer, too wrapped up with his wounded arm. It was throbbing under the bandage like there was an invisible knife being jabbed into it.

"Maybe we can call information or the cops, you know, tell them we need help. Give me your cell phone," Beth told him.

Pastor James looked at her like she was asking him to make wine from water. "What phone? I don't have a phone."

"Why the hell not? Everyone has a cell phone. How can you travel out here and not have a cell phone?"

Pastor James looked defiant, defending his free choice to remain uncontactable.

"I don't have one, all right? Hate the foul things. Don't need one. Never did and never will." He turned to her, his face one of victory. "And if they're so great then why don't you have one?"

Beth pursed her lips. "I did, but I lost it back in New York. I think it fell out of my pocket. I'm on the road. It's not like I can just call and get a new one. I'll have to wait till I get to Maine." She turned her head to stare at him. "Everyone has a cell phone. They just do."

Pastor James was about to reply when his eyes caught something on the road. Beth was still staring at him, her eyes not seeing the object which had strolled onto the highway. She only realized there was a problem when she saw his eyes go wide in fright. Looking forward, her mouth dropped open and she swerved the wheel, trying to avoid the impact that was coming.

A hundred feet down the highway, a large Bull Moose had strolled onto the pavement. It lowered its head, its antlers facing the grille and Beth realized the animal was going to charge her.

As they drew closer and she tried to take evasive action, her mind tried to take in the condition of the moose.

More than a month ago, the moose had been taken down by a hunter, but it hadn't been hunting season yet and when a ranger arrived on the scene, the hunter had taken off, leaving his kill where it had fallen. The moose had laid there ever since. Or until the comet had come into Earth's orbit.

Now the animal was walking around again, and it was very much worse off than before. Half its right side was a caved in gulley, ants and bugs crawling around, mixing with thousands of maggots. Its face was a rotting pile of meat, with white bone peeking through above the eyes and around the jaw. The lips, or lack thereof, were peeled back, exposing the brown teeth, giving the moose a jester-like smile. One eye was completely missing, the other dislodged slightly. But the optical nerve was still attached and somehow the dead moose could still see.

Beth took all this in at a glance as she swerved the car to the right, avoiding the moose by inches. Still the moose tried to strike the Cadillac, the antlers slamming into the driver's side of the car, metal scraping on bone. The car shuddered as it streaked by and then the moose was behind them.

Beth's hands were wrapped around the steering wheel and she slammed on the brakes, not wanting to ditch the car on the shoulder, where there was a slight slope for water drainage when rainfall came.

The engine purred and only Beth and Pastor James' breathing filled the car.

"What the fuck was that?" Pastor James exclaimed, letting his man of the cloth façade slip in his terror.

Beth shook her head, her voice locked in her throat. Swallowing the large knot, her larynx cleared and she managed a whisper.

"A moose?"

Pastor James looked at her with absolute shock.

"A moose? That was no moose, missy; there was only half of it there! Did you see that? There was only half of it 'cause the other half was missing! How in God's name could that be?"

She was about to retort when the sound of hoofs clacking on the highway caused her to look up, into the rearview mirror. The moose was coming for her and the dead animal was now missing half its antlers thanks to its impact with the Cadillac.

"Oh shit, its still back there!" She screamed, flooring the gas pedal, the Cadillac surging forward. The moose tried to catch up, but the car quickly outdistanced the dead animal until it was lost in the dust of the highway.

Beth was breathing hard, her mind racing while she tried to figure out what the hell was going on. Next to her, Pastor James was praying, his mumblings filling the car, only a few of his words making sense.

Her eyes roamed the edge of the highway where it lined the woods and she was shocked to begin to see animals creeping onto the shoulder of the road. As the Cadillac zoomed past, she saw all kinds of woodland creatures, but all had taken on a dark turn. It was like Bambi on acid.

There were field mice and deer, standing next to rabbits and a large cat, which from her studies in school she new was a Canadian Lynx. Then two more cats came out and stood behind the first. They were endangered, but from where she sat it looked like they were doing just fine. That is with the exception all were dead. They were scraggly creatures with ribs showing through their fur. If she had to guess, she would have figured they had starved to death as she knew it had been a tough winter and spring had really taken its time returning.

The Cadillac was moving by the animals before they could get close enough to cause harm, but when Beth glanced into the rearview mirror, she saw the dead creatures move onto the highway. At first they remained still, as if they were watching her leave them, but then she saw them take their first steps after her. But by then she had driven over a slight incline and the parade of dead animals was lost from sight.

"What the hell was that? Did you just see them, too?" Pastor James squeaked as his head turned almost all the way around to see behind him.

"Yeah, I saw it, though I can't believe it. No, there has to be some rational explanation for what we just saw. There has to be." She said the last sentence low, as if she was trying to convince herself it was so.

Taking the curve on the highway, she was able to see the opposite side through the trees. A few trucks passed, their motors rumbling, but other than that it was quiet.

Where were all the other cars? It was midday; surely there should be more people on the road.

On the right side of the road, a sign appeared and she let up on the gas, wanting to read it.

"Exit 9, 1000 feet. DJ's truck stop and diner. Hot food and cold beer; air conditioning," she mumbled to herself.

"What did you say, Sweety Pie?" Pastor James asked. His wrist was throbbing something terrible and he wished he'd been smart enough to have some aspirin in the car.

Beth ignored his statement, concentrating on the sign she'd just seen, the vehicle already passing it.

"That sign, there's a diner at the next exit. They should have a phone there and there will be people there, too. We need to go there, get help for your arm. Maybe they know what's going on."

Pastor James nodded. "Sure, fine, just get me somewhere, please, my arm is killing me."

Beth nodded, for once feeling some sympathy for him. Every now and then, Pastor James let his façade slip and she saw the frail, scared man underneath. But no sooner would this happen, then the veil would descend again, making her despise this so-called preacher she had been foolish enough to take a ride from. She wondered where she would be if she had refused the ride offered to her all those miles back. But then she thought of all the dead animals roaming the highway and decided maybe she was better off where she was. At least she was inside a car, not alone and walking on the highway, fair game to any of the predators who seem to have appeared magically from the woods.

Neither talked for the next three minutes and when the exit appeared, Beth took it, the Cadillac swerving slightly as she took the off ramp a little too fast. At the bottom was a fork.

Left for the diner and right for the nearby town of Atkinson.

She swung left, and was almost struck by a small compact car, which blasted her with its shrill, impotent horn, and then drove off down the road.

The diner was only two minutes off the exit and she pulled into the potholed parking lot. No sooner did she stop the car then she realized the diner wouldn't be any safer than the highway.

Lining the parking lot and moving closer with each passing second, a line of rotting, dead animals flowed out of the woods. The woodland creatures were in all states of decay and a few were so far beyond living Beth couldn't imagine how they managed to move.

A pair of dead squirrels jumped onto the hood of the Cadillac, hissing at her and Pastor James. One of them hopped onto the windshield, its paws scratching at the surface of the glass. It wanted in, only it wasn't bright enough to understand why the clear panel of glass was stopping it from attacking the meat within the vehicle.

Beth panicked, screamed high and long, and turned on the windshield wipers. The wiper blade struck the animal and knocked it to the ground, but the other one quickly took the place of the first. This second squirrel had been dead for weeks, the rear part of its body flattened, a few tread marks still visible in its mottled fur. It had been crushed by a passing car while trying to cross the road across from the diner and had died on the shoulder after dragging itself the twenty feet to safety.

A few small entrails, withered and dry, hung from the underside of its body and brushed across the hood of the Cadillac.

Pastor James jumped back in his seat and began muttering prayers, his eyes glued to the desiccated animal only two feet in front of him.

It wasn't so much the danger of the animal that was so unsettling, as the two humans were like giants to the small, dead animal. No, that wasn't what had both of them cringing in fear.

It was the simple, unbelievable reality that the creature on the hood of the Cadillac was dead. Pure and absolutely dead. There was no doubt about it.

Faced with the unimaginable truth of the situation would knock anyone's world view askew and Beth and Pastor James were no different.

The wiper blades were still going and the second squirrel followed the first to the pavement, the dried body almost floating to the ground.

Beth looked out the windshield and saw more animals coming for them. They had seconds to decide what they were going to do. They either had to run for the diner doors or pull back onto the road and try their luck someplace else.

One look at Pastor James' bloody wound and it was obvious what the answer would be. The man needed medical help. Much more than Beth could provide for him. Already he was looking pale, as if he had caught some kind of flu and was fighting off the infection. He had black bags under his eyes and was perspiring terribly. When he looked at her, she could see his eyes were glazed over, as if he had consumed too much liquor and was now thoroughly plastered.

Besides, inside the diner would be a phone, other people, and perhaps someone who had a handle on what was happening.

Beth turned to Pastor James, her eyes wide with fright, but still filled with determination. She was strong and it didn't take long for her to calm down and face her fears.

"We need to go, Pastor. That diner is our best shot. Especially with your arm like that," she said as she flicked her gaze back out the window. On her left, rabbits, snakes and chipmunks, along with small mice and a few rats were hopping across the parking lot directly towards the Cadillac. To her right, she could see two white-tailed deer, a coyote, three weasels, a couple of voles and a small Black bear, all in similar forms of decomposition, and all were moving towards her location. She snapped her attention back to Pastor James who was shaking his head in denial.

"Yes, we need to go now. Look, I'm going. You can stay here or follow me. I really don't care. But that diner is where I'm going." She sucked in a breath and let it out. "Okay, on three," she said while reaching for the door handle. The engine was off and she dropped the keys in her pocket, despite the fact the vehicle wasn't hers.

Pastor James continued mumbling, but his free hand reached out for the door handle.

"One, two…Three!" Beth yelled, throwing open the car door and jumping out onto the parking lot. Immediately, a few of the closest animals went for her and she dodged two and kicked the others away, already spinning on her heels to head for the diner,

Dashing around the front of the car, she charged forward, her eyes flicking back and forth as the macabre woodland life tried to catch her. Pastor James was moving too, but not as fast as she was. He was an out of shape, middle-aged man and he showed it with each faltering step he took.

A seagull and three pigeons dipped out of the sky to try and scratch out his eyes, and in the brief instant before the dead avians banked away, he saw their exploded abdomens and the missing left eye on one of the pigeons.

"They fly, too?" He mumbled in between the prayers he was chanting, and waved his free hand over his head to keep the birds away from his face.

Beth had made it halfway across the parking lot and was only a few yards from the diner's doors.

Sprinting between two pickup trucks, she was stopped short when a deer's head jumped out at her from head high. There was large a hole in its side and she could see the piece of arrow still sticking out of it, red and dried ichor dripping from the puckered wound.

This deer was in the rear bed of a truck and had been left there while the owner went in to grab something to eat after bagging it in the woods only hours ago. The dead deer's mouth opened wide, and the once cute animal was a vicious image to behold. With nostrils flaring, the teeth dove in, trying to take a bite out of Beth's cheek. Only her quick instincts saved her and her head flew back, like when someone tosses a baseball at your face.

She turned to run the other way, but saw she was surrounded.

Dozens of dead animals were moving towards her, some dragging broken or crushed torsos behind them. She spotted a squirrel which was nothing but a head and front limbs, the rest nothing but a flat piece of flesh. It was what was popularly called a *sail* squirrel.

When an animal became road kill, each and every tire that drove over it after the first slowly flattened the carcass until there was nothing left but something that could be peeled from the road and used like a paper airplane.

Toss it into the wind and watch it sail away on a gentle updraft.

The deer climbed to its feet, air hissing like a worn out steam engine from its punctured lung and tried to bite her again. Pastor James picked the same time to come up behind her, and in his haste to escape the birds, he pushed on her back, moving her into the deer's circumference.

Her hands were spread out in front of her, as if the very air could become solid like a wall and stop her from entering the deer's murderous kill zone.

She saw those off-white teeth and flaring nostrils coming at her and knew in less than a second she would feel the hard teeth sinking into the tender flesh of her face.

Then there was the echo of a thunderous roar and she felt more than heard something go splash, her face becoming wet and the sound of the deer stumbling in the rear of the truck.

She opened her eyes an instant later and instead of seeing teeth coming for her, she saw the headless corpse of the deer stumbling on wobbly legs. Where the neck had connected to the head there was now a jagged, bloody stump. A maroon fluid seeped from the stump, and as she watched, the deer pitched over and crashed into the truck bed, the shocks making the pickup bounce for a few seconds from the dead weight of the carcass.

"Come on there, girl, get a move on, there's more coming behind you!" This came from someone at the diner and she turned her head, blinked, and saw two men standing at the diner's glass doors. One was big, wore a big Stetson hat and carried a large shotgun. Even as she watched, he cracked it in half and took out the spent shell, reached into a pocket and slid another fresh one inside. With practiced ease, he closed the breach and prepared to fire again, now having two rounds at his disposal.

Next to the large man was an average sized man. He was about Beth's age and was cute. He was cute in the way some men didn't realize they were cute. She could tell just by the way he stood, the way his clothes hung on his body and the way he looked at her, his eyes filled with concern. He waved her on, preparing to move across the lot to help her when the larger fellow stopped him with an outstretched hand.

The man with the shotgun raised it and aimed the muzzle at a particularly large group of dead woodland animals, and with a snarl and a grin, fired one shot into the middle of the group. Bits of fur, gobbets of flesh, legs and limbs went flying in all directions, clearing a small path for the younger man. He took the chance given him and darted across the lot, reaching Beth in seconds.

Beth stood watching him as if he had just materialized out of thin air.

Behind her, Pastor James pushed on her back, wanting her to get moving. Only seconds had passed since the deer's head had disappeared in a red mist and she was still trying to figure out what was happening.

The cute man grabbed her left arm and pulled her to him, his face set tight with worry.

"Come on, they won't stay separated for long," he gasped while dragging her across the lot. Pastor James followed her, his free hand holding Beth's shirt like she was his mother and he was a child at the shopping mall who didn't want to get lost.

A Gray fox poked its head out from under a car and nipped at Pastor James ankle. The man yelped in pain and kicked the fox away from him, the furry body spinning tail over head to land on the warm pavement. The animal was up in a second and running back to the man.

Now limping, Pastor James followed Beth and the younger man until they were only a few feet from the diner doors and the large man with the Stetson hat.

The man raised the shotgun and Beth thought she was about to get shot when the younger man yanked her to the side, giving the big man the room he needed.

Another roaring blast filled the parking lot and three rabbits, a beaver, two possum, and a raccoon disintegrated into nothing but red chunks and bits of bone. Seconds later there was the pitter patter of rain as the red mist succumbed to gravity and dropped to the ground. The sickly sweet scent of copper filled the air and Beth scrunched up her nose in distaste.

The big man stepped aside and Beth found herself being pulled through the double glass doors of the diner, Pastor James still holding on to her like a waif in a crowded theatre.

"Come on, get the hell in there; here the dead bastards come again!" The big man screamed. He shouldered the shotgun and began backing up behind the others, eyeing the approaching animals warily. He ducked when a pigeon screamed out of the sky and his eyes went wide when it was followed by a bald eagle, the once majestic avian now a mottled husk of dry bones and feathers. Its once white crown was covered in brown and its legs were missing. If the dead bird tried to land it would end up mimicking an airplane with no landing gear.

Ducking low and turning to the diner, the man ran after the others, belaying his size for one brief moment.

Upon entering the diner, he spun, grabbed the door handles and slammed them closed, threatening to shatter the heavy glass. Three seconds passed until the first dead creature struck the glass, rebounding off it with a high pitched clang. Soon, others were doing the same; rabbits, squirrels and even a bear cub, all whacking their bodies against the glass. But the heavy inch thick glass held.

Deciding there was nothing to do about it, the man drew the shades, hiding the animals attempt at breaking into the diner.

"Now why did you do that, DJ?" Mary Jane asked from near the counter. She was hugging a pile of napkins like they were a stuffed animal, her once placid face now creased with fear and worry.

"Because I can hear the dead bastards, that's why. I don't need to keep lookin' at them."

"But what if they break in?" This came from one of the truckers.

DJ shrugged. "Then they get in." He hefted the shotgun, cracked it in half and slid two more fresh shells into the breach, dropping the empties to the floor of the diner like discarded empty beer cans at a kegger. "But if they do, I'll make sure to send more than a few of them back to Hell before they get me." To illustrate his point, he snapped the shotgun back together and made sure it was cocked.

The younger man was still next to Beth and he touched her arm.

"You okay? That was pretty damn close if you ask me." He held out his hand, a lopsided grin on his lips. "I'm Jake, by the way."

Beth was shaking slightly, her mind still racing, and she held out her hand on instinct. "Bethany. Or Beth." She nodded to herself. "Yes, Beth is what people call me."

Jake nodded, his grin turning into a full fledged smile. "Beth it is." He pulled his eyes away from her and looked to Pastor James. The man was leaning against a table and one of the patrons of the diner was helping him. Jake moved over to the perspiring man, his eyes taking in his wounded wrist.

"Hey there, mister, you don't look so good. You okay?"

"Okay…Okay?" Pastor James paused, sucking in a good breath of air. "Why in the Lord's name does everyone always ask that? My God, I could have a house fall on me and there will always be one idiot who'll ask you if you're okay." He let out a breath and sucked in another one. "No, I'm not okay. A damn dog bit me and then something got me on the ankle."

Jake bent down so he could see the man's ankles.

"Really? Let me see if I can help."

He reached out to touch Pastor James's leg and the man of God nodded it was all right. Jake reached out, sliding the pant leg up and winced at the sight. There was a good half inch chunk of the man's flesh missing, blood seeping out of the wound to flow into the man's shoes. Jake figured the shoe would squish when he walked, like he had stepped in a deep puddle of water. Turning, he called to Mary Jane.

"Hey, gorgeous, can I have a couple of those napkins? I think this guy needs them more than you right now."

Mary Jane looked up, and after a second her eyes focused and she nodded, walking around the counter to give Jake some of the napkins. Grinning up to her, he quickly wrapped them around the wound, frowning at the weird lines which seemed to seep from the edge of the bite. But he ignored it, and wrapped the ankle as tightly as he could. When he finished, he stood up, wiping his hands on his pants.

"That should hold you. At least until we can get you to the hospital."

Beth perked up at that and moved a step closer to Jake. The glass doors were rattling like drums and she tried to ignore them; as hard as that was.

"That's why we came here. We need help. A phone."

DJ snickered. "A phone? Hell, honey, the phone went out over an hour ago and no one can get cell reception in these mountains worth a damn. One of these days they said they're gonna put a cell tower around here, but so far it's all been talk."

"So there's no way to tell anyone we need help?" Beth asked.

DJ nodded. "I'm afraid so, honey, but don't worry, you're safe in here for now."

The doors rattled again, a sickening crash that had everyone in the diner jumping.

DJ went back to the double doors and opened the shade, frowning at what he saw. A midsized moose had tried to ram the doors, and with those horns it was a good chance the glass could be breached. In the parking lot, the headless deer he'd shot was now walking around, bumping into other animals and cars. The moose prepared to try again with the glass.

"Why you no good dead bastard," DJ mumbled under his breath. Unlocking the door, he kicked a few animals who tried to get past him and shoved the barrel of the shotgun out through the crack. When he had the moose in his gun sight, he fired, sending a barrage of pellets straight into dead moose's neck. The head was severed from the body and the body went one way and the head straight down. The legs kicked the decapitated head away and the headless body moved off, not realizing it was dead for real without a head.

The moose ended up finding the headless deer and the two got stuck, neither moving out of the way. The severed stumps pushed on one another while the mindless carcasses moved about on autopilot.

Slamming the doors closed again, DJ shook his head.

"Now if that ain't the craziest damn thing I've ever seen." He closed the shades on the door and turned to Beth and Pastor James, who was whimpering as one of the patrons helped him with his wrist wound.

"Well, you two, welcome to the party. Get comfortable; because I think you're gonna be here for a while."

A small, dead mouse scurried near his boots, the little bugger sneaking past him when he slammed the doors shut. He lifted his boot high and stomped down on the undead critter, flattening it with a silent screech.

Wiping the sole of his boot against a small hump on the floor, he grinned at his new patrons.

"Yes, sir, a little while indeed."

4

TRAPPED

Bᴇᴛʜ ʟᴏᴏᴋᴇᴅ ᴀᴛ the faces surrounding her, taking in each visage slowly.

In a far cubby was a small, balding man with a pair of thin eyeglasses perched on his nose. His face was filled with worry and his large forehead was awash with perspiration. He was hugging a book, but from where Beth stood, she couldn't see what kind it was. In the cubby next to the small man were a couple. Just by the way they sat she knew they were married. They sat with a full foot separating them from each other, as if they unconsciously wanted to get away from one another. They looked to be in their late forties or early fifties.

In the booth next to the older couple was another couple, though these two were much younger. These two sat nice and close together, even their hands intertwined and Beth knew immediately they were married; only these two had been married for a short time. In the booth next to the younger couple was a plain looking woman with brown hair with the features of a mouse. The second Beth's gaze met the woman's returning look, however, she looked away. Beth continued on, and in the next booth were three truckers; beer bellies and ball caps completing the picture. She turned her head to see the younger man looking at her. She smiled and he moved towards her, leaving Pastor James to wallow in misery.

"Hey," he said simply.

"Hey, yourself," she smiled. "Thanks for saving me back there. I really appreciate it."

He smirked and scratched his ear, "Aww, it was nothin."

He stared at his feet for a few seconds, the awkward silence weighing down on them. Then a man in an apron came out of the back of the kitchen with two cups of ice water. He handed one to Beth and the other to Jake.

Jake took the cup and smiled at the man. "Thanks, Carlos, you read my mind."

Carlos nodded, mumbled something in Spanish and then went back to the rear of the diner.

Jake drank deeply while Beth did the same, askance of him. She was still pretty shook up from everything that had happened, but these people seemed to act like they were safe in the diner and the feeling was rubbing off on her.

"That's Carlos. He washes the dishes here. Good guy."

Beth nodded.

Mary Jane moved next to Beth, eyeing the younger girl. She had been talking to DJ in hushed voices and now she walked away looking upset. When she was in easy speaking distance of Beth, she smiled at her, pointing to the Pastor behind her.

"You're friend doesn't look so good, honey," Mary Jane told her with a wave of her arm.

Beth shot a glance at Pastor James and nodded, finishing her water in a few heavy gulps.

"He's not my friend. He's just a grabby guy who gave me a ride. He got bit by a dog on the road. It was the weirdest thing." She snickered, then. "Well, maybe not as weird as what's going on around here and outside." She gestured to the front of the diner, the glass doors still shaking from dead animal carcasses striking it. "Just what the hell *is* going on around here?"

DJ took that as his cue to speak up again and he strolled over to her, the shotgun resting over a large shoulder. When he was close to her, she scrunched up her nose. The large man reeked of beef jerky and cigar smoke.

"What's going on, little lady, is it's the goddamn end of the world, that's what."

"What the fuck are you talking about, DJ?" Jake hissed. He finished his water and leaned forward to set it on the counter. Wanting something to do, anything that resembled normalcy, Mary Jane scooped up the cup and carried it to the bus tray. Then she moved away to talk to the patrons, all sitting in their booths. The truckers were out of their seats, moving about the diner now while the two married couples stayed seated. The mousy woman and the small man with the book also stayed seated; his eyes only on the parking lot. A dead bird flew into the glass near his head and he jumped up, then dropped back down. He looked to see if anyone saw him and the tried to act brave, which he was failing miserably.

DJ repositioned the shotgun and glared down at Jake. The big man had a good foot of height on Jake, but the smaller man held his ground, the two men resembling David and Goliath.

"I'm talking about the end, Jake. The goddamn end of it all. Look outside. What the hell do you see? Those are dead animals, people!" He looked around the diner, his eyes flashing with the wan light. "Those are goddamn, fucking dead animals. Did you see that moose? I took its damn head off and it kept on walking around. And last time I checked, a moose ain't like a damn chicken. When you take off its head it's supposed to die." He shook his head. "No way, people, there's something happening here, something so messed up that the dead are friggin' walking. At least thank God it's only the animals."

"What do you mean by that, DJ?" This came from Bubba, who was sliding closer to DJ. He wanted in on the conversation.

"What do I mean? Shit, Bubba. I mean that so far only the animals are walking around, but what happens if this shit affected people, too? We could have a shitload of zombies on our hands."

"DJ, what are you talking about?" Mary Jane asked, wiping the counter with a moist towel. "That's ridiculous. Zombies are fictional characters, like Dracula. They're in the movies and books, they aren't real."

"So far," Bubba said. "Yeah, DJ, yeah, you might be right. But what can we do about it?"

DJ shook his head. "Don't know, but if any of those zombie bastards get near here, I'll fill them full of holes."

"Make sure to get 'em in the head, DJ! They say that's how you kill 'em!" This came from Wilson, one of the truck drivers. Wilbur was askance of him and he chuckled at his remark, receiving a scornful look from DJ.

"Shut the hell up, both of you. You'll see. When the zombies come, it'll be me saving your sorry asses. I'm the one who got the firepower to take them out!"

"You're not the only one who has a gun, DJ. Hell, this is New Hampshire, not Massachusetts," Bubba said with a scowl. He reached around his back and pulled forth a .38 snub-nose, the finish as black as coal.

DJ only grunted, looking at the handgun like he was comparing penis sizes with the trucker.

Jake moved away from DJ, finished with hearing his ravings. He walked up to an empty booth and gazed out into the parking lot. There were more than three hundred animals moving about, all flowing back and forth. Some were crawling on cars and trucks and others were snapping at one another. He watched a small bear cub, half of its side missing and rotted away, fighting with a pair of possums for some small scrap of meat. They were really going at it until an eagle appeared overhead, swooped down low and plucked the meat from the cub's jaws. Then it soared away, catching an updraft.

Jake only saw it for a moment, but he saw the half eaten head and maggot ridden wings. How the avian was flying was anyone's guess.

Beth joined him, her face filled with concern.

"What the hell is happening here? I just wanted to go to Maine. That's all. Why's all this happening?" Her eyes filled with tears and she wiped them away, not wanting to cry in front of strangers. Jake didn't know if he was pushing his luck, but he reached around her with his right hand, hugging her gently. Unexpectedly, she leaned against him and placed her head on his shoulder. She needed someone to hold her, and at the moment, even a stranger would do. Her legs began to feel weak with the adrenalin seeping away and she moved out of his arm, sliding into a nearby booth. Jake decided to join her and sat down across from her. For a few moments, neither person spoke, while all around them the patrons of the diner talked and argued. The older couple wanted to leave, the woman saying they should make a run for their car. The older man was against it and the woman said he never agreed with her anyway, and why should now be any different, despite the fact it could cost them their lives. The younger couple was talking about their family, wondering if their loved ones were okay. The truckers and DJ had moved next to Mary Jane and they were talking together; DJ yelling to be heard over the others.

Beth looked up from the table and saw Jake was looking at her with a compassionate grin. She wiped a stray tear away with the back of her hand and sniffed.

"What? What's wrong? What are you looking at me like that? Never seen a girl cry before?"

He shrugged. "I'm looking at you because you're upset. Hell, who wouldn't be? Don't worry, we'll be all right. Help has got to come for us sooner or later."

She nodded, hoping he was right, while behind her, two booths over, Pastor James moaned with pain as his wounds sent pins and needles of agony through his body. His head rolled back and forth and his eyes fluttered as the man dealt with the anguish of his wounds, the pain so intense it was like his veins were full of gasoline and someone had struck a match.

"Yeah, help will come," she said, "but will it be in time for all of us?"

5

BAD DECISIONS

THE ENEMY WITHIN

"HEY, THE TV's on! Hey, everybody; the cables on again!" Mary Jane called out to the occupants of the diner. More than three hours had passed since Beth and Pastor James had arrived, and despite the constant bombardment of the animals on the thick glass lining the front of the diner, a lull of boredom had fallen over everyone. Once the initial expectancy of danger was passed, eventually heightened senses finally succumbed to the lack of stimulation and relaxed again. Unfortunately, there was nothing to do inside the diner but sit, talk, eat or drink.

DJ had been running a tab for everyone, the thrifty diner owner not about to just give the food away. He figured once the crisis was over, he would still have bills to pay, so every cup of coffee, every donut eaten, every sandwich devoured, was accounted for. Mary Jane had taken on the menial task of keeping the tabs up to date, marking down the price of the food and the item taken.

As one group, everyone gathered around the front counter, gazing up at the nineteen-inch television.

"I can't hear what they're saying; turn the damn thing up, Mary Jane!" DJ snapped as he craned his neck to see the screen. Next to him, was Carlos. The small Spanish man was silent. His English was atrocious and he only used it when absolutely necessary. Usually, Jake would give him hand signals of what he needed him to do, the shorthand between the two growing from months of working side by side, now making the two function well as a team.

Picking up the remote control, Mary Jane turned up the volume, and in seconds the television was loud enough to quell the banging on the glass doors, only Pastor James' moans still being heard inside the diner. The wounded man had been going downhill. His temperature was hot, then cold, and his complexion had taken on a pale sheen. One of the truckers said it was probably shock, but no one was a doctor and couldn't say for sure. Pastor James was in the last booth near the rear of the diner, lying out on a bench; his legs over the side.

"What's happening? What are they saying?" This came from Ruth. Her husband was behind her, also watching the screen. Her question went unanswered, everyone's attention on the television.

"Shut up and listen and you'll find out," DJ snapped at her, irritated. The newscaster was talking and he wanted to hear.

Ruth looked indignant and flashed her husband a dirty look.

"Walter, are you going to let him talk to me like that?"

Walter shrugged. "He's right, Ruth. Shut up and you'll hear the TV."

Ruth, annoyed, turned around in a huff of anger, but her eyes went to the television again, her voice now silent.

On the screen was a pretty Asian woman in her late twenties. From anyone living in New Hampshire, it was obvious she was standing in the middle of downtown Portsmouth. All around her people could be seen running here and there. Behind her, a three car pile up was filling the screen with smoke and a horn blared from somewhere off in the distance. From the camera's angle, small shapes flittered between the legs of the running pedestrians, but the camera wasn't able to focus on them, as the cameraman had his lense aimed at the young reporter.

"This is Michelle Takinawa, reporting from downtown Portsmouth, where a state of emergency is under way. For some unknown reason, animals have gone on the attack, some appearing to be either dead or about to die. We have had reports of rats and mice spewing from the sewers in New York City and dogs and cats actually unearthing themselves from shallow graves in backyards of homes all across the United States. The President has already planned to address the nation on this seemingly unbelievable crisis and is even now in conference with some of our nation's top scientists and pathologists.

New York, Boston and Chicago are told to be only a few of the hardest hit cities, as the rat population of the sewers is larger there due to the size of the cities. Somehow, the dead carcasses have returned to life and are now pouring out of the sewers in what we believe is in a search for human food. Though at the moment we can't confirm this. We will stay on this story for as long as it takes to get to the bottom of it. Here at channel 12, you can count on the best up to date minute news…"

She was cut off then, when an orange and yellow shape lunged at her face from off camera. The cameraman panned down as the young woman went to the sidewalk, her microphone falling from panicked hands. Instead of helping her, the cameraman zoomed in, making sure to get every bloody and grizzly second of footage.

"Oh, man, I'm gonna get a Pulitzer for this," a voice said from off camera.

Meanwhile, the woman was screaming for help.

An alley cat had jumped on her, its mottled and bloody hide covered in dried blood. The animal had been dead for more than a week and maggots festered under its fur. Its claws were razor sharp, its teeth still deadly, and the cat used them, sinking its teeth into the woman's neck. The reporter let out a screech while wrapping her hands around the spastic animal, her hands sinking deep into the fur, as she tried desperately to yank the cat away from her, but all she succeeded in doing was to skin the animal. Its dried fur separated from its body, tearing like wet paper and the skeleton and tendons glistened in the light of the day. Claws scratched at her eyes and one punctured the left orb, the woman going blind instantly in that eye. The cameraman never faltered, never tried to help her; only laughed at the terrific footage he was getting. The cat worried its fangs into the woman's neck, and soon enough, it struck pay dirt, severing the carotid artery. The young, Asian reporter began to bleed out, squealing like a stuck pig, her thrashing growing slower until her arms fell to her sides like dead weights. The cameraman pulled back then and suddenly the camera spun around, the lens going wide. Coming down the street was more than a thousand rats, mice, ferrets, some large snakes, and a few dogs, all in similar states of decomposition. The camera began moving backwards, and then the lens shifted down as the cameraman began to run. The sidewalk blurred by in a flash and the man's heavy breathing could be heard. Stains on the sidewalk showed of where other attacks had happened and once or twice a stray limb or foot could be seen in the screen before the cameraman had moved on. Then the man tripped, the camera sliding across the pavement. No sooner did he fall then a score of blurred shapes ran past the lens and flowed over the man. From the angle of the camera, lying on its side, the diner patrons had a good view of the man as he was swallowed by a sea of animals, all tearing and biting. His face was peeled off while he shrieked; batting away each carcass only to have three more replace it. When his struggles waned, the screen finally changed, now the anchorman in the newsroom staring back at the camera and the world watching in shock.

The man was speechless and a voice told him to start talking, that they were live. He cleared his throat, wiped his forehead with a sleeve and began talking; droning on about the state of emergency and how all citizens should remain indoors, and stay out of the city for the time being.

DJ moved to Mary Jane and grabbed the remote from her, aiming it at the screen and turning it off.

"Hey, why'd you do that?" Bubba asked, annoyed.

"Because we saw all we're gonna see; that's why. If the shit's that bad in the city and other places, too, then we're on our own out here. Hell, we're probably safer here anyway."

"Safer? Are you serious? Look at all those bastards out there," Wilson said, some of the others agreeing. Others were stark silent, their faces impassive after witnessing the slaughter of two people by something out of their nightmares.

Ruth turned to her husband, her face filled with panic.

"Walter, we need to get out of here. We need to get home. What about Fluffy? He's all alone."

"Oh, for Christ sake's, Ruth, the damn cat is fine. Hell, by the way things are going, he'll probably out live us all."

"No, Walter, we need to leave here before it's too late. Our car is right outside the doors. We can make a run for it, we can make it."

Walter frowned, then bit his lower lip as he gave it some thought. He wanted to leave, too, though he would never admit to Ruth she was right. He had learned a long time ago that marriage was a constant struggle for dominance, a struggle he often won, but usually lost. But the truth was he had been thinking the same thing. The animals outside the glass were slow. They could run to their car, get in, and be gone before any of them could reach them. The trick was to get past the ones at the doors. His eyes roamed the diner and then he saw the exit sign of the rear exit. Of course, they could go out the back door and run around the building. He could even ask if some of the others could bang on the glass doors, distract the animals while they ran for it. Besides, he wanted to get home and check on his mother. She was only a block from his house and he knew she must be terrified with everything that was happening. She was getting up there in age and didn't always understand things anymore. If she was foolish enough to go outside…well, he tried not to think about it. He had always been somewhat of a mother's boy, and that was what had probably attracted him to Ruth. She shared many traits with his mother, perhaps too many.

"Fine, Ruth, we can leave, but first I have to talk to the owner over there."

"About what? Walter, every second we waste is a moment too long."

"Ruth, just give me a second, all right? Christ, we need to have a plan. We can't just go running out there, there's too many of those things waiting in the parking lot. But I have an idea."

She opened her mouth to protest and he pointed a finger at her face, threatening her to stop.

Suddenly, she did. She was getting her way and decided not to push her luck. If Walter wanted to take an extra second she would give him this one thing. Her mother said sometimes you had to give the man an inch so he didn't take a foot. Her mother was a battered woman, but Ruth had never seemed to let that stop her from listening to her advice, though her mother's marriage was a shambles until she had died a few years ago of a stroke.

Her father was now remarried and living with a woman half his age and Ruth hadn't spoken to him since the wake. The bastard had defiled her mother's memory as far as she was concerned.

With nothing to do but wait for Walter to finish with whatever he wanted to do, she moved away from the counter, her mind racing to take in what she had seen on the television, while thoughts of her precious Fluffy waiting alone in her home danced across her mind.

*   *   *

Pastor James moaned yet again and Wilbur looked up from his cup of coffee to scowl.

"Will you shut the hell up! Christ, you're driving me crazy!"

"He can't help it, mister, the poor man is sick," Liz said from the next booth. Matt was by her side, having returned with two plates of pie. Neither of them was that hungry, their stomachs in knots over what was happening to them and the world, but Matt said they needed to eat.

Wilbur turned slightly so the top part of his head could be seen over the booth.

"No shit, miss, but that still doesn't change the fact the guy is driving me crazy." Wilbur crooked his neck so he could find DJ and he called out. "Hey, DJ, can't we put that guy somewhere in the back of the diner where he won't make so much noise?"

Liz made a disgusted sound inside her throat. "Oh my God, that's barbaric. The man's wounded. He needs our help, not to be tossed into the back like a bag of trash."

Pastor James moaned again and Wilbur smashed his hand on the table, causing the coffee cup and the salt and pepper shakers to jump.

"I don't care! I want him away from me, damn it. DJ, hey, DJ!" Wilbur searched the diner for the owner and then the trucker saw Jake in a far booth and he shifted his attentions to the younger man. "Hey,

Jake, how 'bout helping me get that guy in the back. I could use some peace and quiet for a while."

Jake turned to Beth and gestured to Pastor James.

"How 'bout it, Beth? Can we move him to the back? There's a cot set up there for when I have to stay late and wax the floors. We could put him in there."

Beth shrugged. "You don't have to ask me, Jake. I barely know the guy. It's fine with me."

Jake nodded, stood up and called Wilbur over to him.

"Okay, Wilbur, you got your wish, grab someone else and we can move him to the back room."

"Hot damn, finally some peace and quiet."

"You people are horrible; he's wounded for God sakes!" Liz said again.

"Fine, lady, then why don't you go stay with him, huh? I don't see you doin; anything but flappin' your mouth."

Liz looked insulted and Matt began to stand up. Wilbur turned his attention to Matt, an ugly sneer on his lips.

"You don't want to do that, pal, believe me. Just leave it alone and so will I," Wilbur warned him. "I'm not lookin' for trouble, just some peace and quiet."

Matt studied the large trucker's face, and saw no malice there, so he decided he would do just that. If Wilbur wasn't pushing the issue then neither would he. Lowering himself back down, he spoke softly to Liz, telling her to mind her own business.

Wilbur stood up and jumped when a bird hit the glass wall of the diner, the small avian splattering against the glass to slide down like a piece of wet spaghetti. After the bird was gone from view, a small slime trail remained. Wilbur, now a little more serious, turned away from the glass and moved towards Jake. On the way, he passed Wilson and slapped the man on the back. After filling Wilson in on what he wanted, the two men joined Jake.

"Okay, you get the legs and I'll get the head," Wilbur told the other two men.

With a few pulls and heaves, the three men managed to carry Pastor James into the back room, the entire time the wounded man was moaning, his wails filling the diner. Upon setting him on the cot, the two truckers left and Jake took a second to check on the man's wounds. Unwrapping the fetid bandage, he saw the large tear in his wrist was black, with a dark ichor seeping from it. The smaller wound on his ankle was no better. Thin blue lines spread off from the gash to crawl up his leg, the rest lost under his pants. Jake shook his head, grabbed some more bandages from the small first aid kit and quickly dressed the wounds yet again. After putting a liberal amount or hydrogen peroxide on them, he sealed them tightly. The old, saturated bandages he tossed in a plastic bag and dropped in the trash, his nose wrinkling at the sickly odor.

Pastor James was out of it, the man sleeping again. When he wasn't moaning, he was sleeping and even a layman knew the man needed medical help fast. Pastor James' complexion was pale; making the man look like he was a ghost and his face was covered with a sheen of perspiration, his cheeks bloated like he was filling with water. His lips trembled and his eyelids fluttered and Jake wondered if he was going to die.

Though not wanting the man to die, the truth was Jake didn't know him, and so there was only so much caring he could send the man. Deciding he had done all he could for the hapless man, he exited the storeroom, leaving the door open a crack. He shut off the light in the hallway and made his way back to the front of the building. On his way, he passed Carlos in the kitchen. The man was cutting lettuce, acting as if nothing was happening. Upon hearing Jake, the man looked up, waved with his lettuce-covered hand and went back to work. Jake nodded, said a quick hello, and continued on.

Two things happened at the same time he entered the front of the diner. The first was the power went out. It was like someone had flicked all the circuit breakers at the same time. There was a lull for a few seconds, the silence ominous after always hearing the walk-in, small refrigerator, soda machines and other electrical appliances that make up a working diner. Jake entered the diner and saw faces in the gloom. There was still plenty of sunlight and it filtered through the shades over the glass windows. The second thing to happen was the argument that broke out between Walter and DJ. The older man was demanding to leave the diner and DJ was doing his best to stop him. Jake stopped in the shadows of the hallway leading to the rear of the diner and listened to the two men, the other patrons doing the same. Jake had to admit, though DJ was an asshole, the large man was doing his best to change Walter's mind and make the man stay.

"You're a goddamn idiot, pal, you know that? It's death out there. Stay in here with us until help arrives. The power will be back on soon enough, you'll see. Probably just some asshole hit one of the telephone poles with his car out on the highway."

Walter shook his head, adamant. "Thank you for your words, but my wife and I want to leave. She's worried about our home and my mother needs me. I'm sorry, but I've made up my mind. The only question is, will you help me or will you stand in my way?"

DJ sighed, his eyes scanning the other faces of the people in the diner. The young couple was in their booth, minding their own business and the truckers were hovering near the front doors, watching the animals move about. The small man with the bird book was still in his booth, hugging his book like it was a life preserver, as was the brown haired woman, and Mary Jane was a few feet away, watching the tableaux play out. DJ made eye contact with her and his eyebrows went up in a quizzical look. She shrugged; her way of saying she had no answer for him.

Shaking his head, he waved the older man away.

"Fine, pal, do whatever you want. As long as you're not risking anyone else's lives in here, I'll do what I can."

Walter nodded, pleased he had won. He turned to Ruth with a victorious grin on his face and she looked back blandly. She wasn't impressed. Hell, whatever Walter did never impressed her anymore.

Struck down by her gaze, he turned back to DJ, the smile now gone from his lips. "Okay, here's what I thought we could do," he said and filled DJ in on his idea. DJ nodded, frowning a lot and other times shaking his head. But in the end these two were strangers to him, and if they wanted to leave, who was he to argue. While Walter and DJ worked out how the couple was going to escape the diner, the glass doors and walls of the building were continually struck by the animated carcasses of the dead animals, their milky fluids spreading across the glass like thrown eggs on Halloween.

*　　*　　*

Ten minutes later, the back door of the diner swung open and Walter's head appeared. The rear lot was empty, only a few dead animals skulking around near the back corner of the building. Walter spied a small deer close by with a large gaping hole in its side, intestines hanging out like garland on Christmas, and he waited for the animal to move away.

When it was as clear as he thought it could get, he stepped outside, Ruth right behind him.

Turning around, he looked at Jake, who was doing his part to help in the older man's plan.

"Okay, so you tell DJ to shoot a line for us and we'll do the rest," Walter said.

Jake shook his head slightly, not agreeing in the least.

"You two are crazy, man. Stay here, help will come."

Walter waved the suggestion away.

"No, we've been through this; my wife and I need to get home. Thank you for everything." He grinned then. "And thanks for lunch, that burger was delicious."

Jake smiled wanly, the odd comment seemed out of place considering what the older man was about to do. He reached out his hand for Walter and the older man took it.

"Good luck, for what it's worth."

Walter shook Jake's hand, pumping twice. "I'll take it, Jake. Right now I can use all the luck I can get. But we'll be fine. Our car is right near the front door. We'll be there in a second. Hell, they won't even know we're there until it's too late to attack us."

"Walter, will you shut up and come on? I don't like being out here," Ruth said, studying her surroundings warily. A milk snake scurried up to her foot and tried to bite her, but couldn't get past her sneaker. The rear portion of the snake was half eaten, making it resemble a worn shoelace, with only a few threads still hanging on. Ruth kicked it away with a shiver.

"Fine, Ruth, fine, let's go before we're seen. We don't know how smart those animals are, and I don't want to find out."

With a nod to Jake, Walter took Ruth's hand and the two began moving away from the rear of the diner towards the front. Jake watched the couple for another moment, and with a slight frown of concern, closed the back door again. It had already been established the doors would not be opened again. If Walter and Ruth tried to get back in and they had a shitload of animals on their ass, the doors would stay closed or else risk the threat of the dead animals getting inside the diner.

Walter led Ruth to the front corner of the building and stopped as he surveyed the parking lot. Suddenly his idea didn't seem so bright. The lot was filled with all sizes and shapes, every one of the animals in some sort of decomposition. A small rabbit hopped by, only its lack of eyes keeping it from seeing the fleeing couple.

"I don't know about this, Ruth, maybe we should try and go back. I didn't see this many of them when we were inside the diner."

"No, Walter, we have to get home, my baby needs me," Ruth told him, pleading about her cat. There was something in her eyes. Something Walter hadn't seen in a long time, but it made him cave in. For just a moment, he saw the woman he'd fell in love with and married all those years ago.

"Fine, Ruth, but let's do this quick." He looked around for something to use as a weapon, but the ground was sparse. He regretted not bringing anything from inside the diner, but he wasn't a warrior, never had been. He was the kind of man who would turn the other cheek.

Deciding a weapon didn't matter, as the goal was to get to his car and get out of the area, he reached into his pocket and pulled out his keys, prepared for the dash to the car. Making sure he had the correct key in his hand, he turned to Ruth, nodded he was ready, and the two took off at a gallop, trying to move fast but stay hidden.

They made it to the first parked car near the front of the diner before their escape was knocked askew.

Ruth, running unevenly, stepped on what was once a squirrel, but was now a rotting pile of maggots and mottled fur. Her foot went out from under her like she had stepped on a banana and her entire body went into the air. Walter, still holding onto her, was thrown against another car parked two spaces from his own and the sound of his body bouncing off the metal panel was enough to alert every animal in the parking lot they had company.

Ruth landed hard on the ground, her breath leaving her in a whoosh. Walter was in better shape from their screw-up, but that only meant he saw what was happening, Ruth was still oblivious as she lay by his feet

Almost as if someone had clapped their hands for attention, every single animal and rodent turned as one towards the hapless couple. The bombardment of the front doors ceased and all eyes turned to Walter and Ruth.

Three ticks of the clock went by before the first howling scream left fetid jaws and the entire ensemble of dead creatures spun, and then charged at the two already backpedaling couple.

Walter helped Ruth to her feet and struggled to pull her back with him, but their legs became tangled in one another in their haste. Before they had gone a yard, the first animal was upon them; a small Black bear with razor sharp teeth, and a miasma of fetid breath that had Walter gagging on his own bile. The bear ripped him open from groin to neck, spilling his entrails onto the parking lot, and causing the greasy, bloody ropes to steam in the noonday sun. Ruth saw this and screamed, long and loud, but her shout was short-lived when a small sparrow flew straight into her mouth, only its small tail feathers visible between her lips as the small bird burrowed down her throat, blocking her air supply to slowly suffocate her.

Her face turned a pale blue and her hands claws at the air, then at her throat, as she tried to suck in one last gasp of oxygen. Then she was attacked from below, rodents, snakes, a Gray fox, and a few possums climbing up her legs and swarming over her body. A few scurried under her clothing, making her look like she was morphing into some hideous creature. Then the bumps containing animals began to turn red as the creatures burrowed into her flesh, seeking the tasty organs within.

Both Walter and Ruth dropped to the ground, writhing in their anguish as they were fed on from the inside out. Intestines were pulled away, a few field mice doing their best to take their share, but no sooner had the small rodents moved away a few feet, then a dead avian would swoop in from above and snatch the vermillion prizes from their small paws.

Both human beings were enveloped by fur and feathers, their legs kicking a steady staccato of death on the hardtop, but soon those subsided and the couple succumbed to death.

Half a dozen yards away, DJ, Jake, and a few of the other patrons all stood at the glass doors and walls of the diner, watching the visceral tableaux of death before them. From their vantage point, they could only see the twitching feet of the slaughtered couple. Then a spreading pool of blood appeared, slowly meandering across the pavement as it found cracks and gulleys to follow. Immediately, some of the smaller animals began lapping up the viscous fluid, sucking in the rich, warm plasma like it was manna from Heaven.

"Why didn't you do like the guy asked, DJ?" Jake asked. "You said you'd clear a path for them."

DJ nodded. "Yeah, I did tell him that. But I also said as long as it was safe to open the doors. Did you see what happened when that woman fell down? There was no way to save them, Jake. No matter how many times I fired at those dead bastards. Shit, I told him it was suicide, and now everyone knows I'm right."

Jake's face took on a look of anger. "Well, I'm so glad you were proved right, DJ. I wouldn't want you to have to admit you were wrong."

Jake was the first to turn away, disgusted by the sight of the carnage outside and DJ's attitude. But it was something more. By seeing what had happened to the couple, he knew that could be all their fates if the animals managed to break into the diner. And that was something he didn't want to think about. Beth was still in a nearby booth, the woman not wanting to see the older couple make a break for it, and he went over to her, sitting down next to her. Her hands were crossed on the table and he reached out and touched her pinky finger, unsure if he should hold her hand. She answered his query by immediately grasping his hand, squeezing tightly. He nodded to her and the two sat together, for the moment, remaining silent.

Across the diner, the other patrons moved away from the doors and windows and DJ became the sole viewer. His eyes couldn't be pulled away from the four bloody feet, now shoeless, lying prone on the pavement, and he closed his eyes for a moment, trying to push the terrible pictures still remaining there. When that Black bear had ripped Walter open, well, he had never seen anything like that in his entire life.

Five minutes went by, and a few of the animals left the two bodies, moving back to the diner doors. Immediately they began pummeling the doors, only their small carcasses stopping them from gaining entry.

Inside the diner, the patrons went about their business of worrying about their fate and trying to remain calm.

Beth climbed out of the booth and walked around, hugging her body as she thought about where she was and what was happening. It was all just so fantastic. Her eyes spotted the payphone on the far wall and she walked over to it. Dropping a quarter into the coin slot, she lifted the receiver to her ear, and dialed 911. She already knew what she would hear, but something inside her had her try anyway.

"Please stay on the line and we will be with you shortly. If this is an emergency, please dial 911," the recorded voice said, then immediately looped and began again.

She held the phone to her ear for a full five minutes, never moving, almost never blinking. Inside herself, she wanted to scream, a small part of her sliding into the brink of despair she has been feeling ever since arriving at the diner.

Finally, Jake came up behind her and gently took the phone from her hand. He hung it back up and then gently turned her around, looking into her blank gaze. Slowly, her gaze focused on him and she stared at him, her upper lip trembling. Then the dam broke and she began to cry, long and hard. Jake pulled her against his chest and hugged her, muttering soothing words into her ear. The two stayed like that for a long time, while the other patrons tried to ignore them, wanting to give them their moment of privacy.

But the moment was soon to be broken when out of the rear of the diner, Pastor James stumbled out. His complexion was so pale he looked like he was wearing white pancake makeup and his mouth hung slack and to the side like he was a drooling idiot, his jowls swinging back and forth. Only a dull moan left his lips and his head swiveled back and forth like he was being controlled by a five-year-old with a remote control handset. His eyes spotted Beth and he went to her, his hips whacking the tables and booths, a few of the patrons yelling out in annoyance.

If it wasn't for Wilbur, who stopped Pastor James, things might have gone a lot differently, but luck was there for Beth, and just before Pastor James could grab her and do God knows what, Wilbur stepped between them and held out a hand to block Pastor James' path.

"Buddy, you look like shit. Why don't you go back and lay down?" Wilbur told him.

Pastor James never slowed, never even paused. When Wilbur stepped in front of him, the pale-faced man's eyes and head swiveled to follow the hand now promptly displayed in front of him. Like a striking Cobra, his head darted down and his teeth clamped down onto two of Wilbur's fingers, severing them with a sickening crack that had every person in the diner looking up. No sooner did the fingers crunch, then Wilbur screamed long and loud, his voice reaching falsetto proportions. Pastor James worried at the fingers and came back with two nubs protruding from his mouth like newborn seedlings springing from the earth on a cool spring morning.

Blood shot from the severed nubs to spray across the diner, catching Beth, Jake and a few others in its crimson spray. Matt and Liz had been sitting in their booth, minding their own business, and now they were baptized with blood, the warm, sticky fluid covering them from head to chest.

Wilbur, screaming in pain and shock, ran away to be lost in the rear of the diner, near the back rooms and bathrooms.

Pastor James swallowed the severed digits whole and then went back for more, a guttural growl escaping his bloodied lips.

Before he could chase after Wilbur for more, another belching gunshot filled the diner, filling the air with smoke. The side of Pastor James chest exploded outward, bathing the two booths behind him in gore and blood. DJ walked over to the still standing body and was shocked to see Pastor James hadn't gone down yet. The man wobbled on unsteady legs, ignored the gaping wound in his side and then reached in, took a hold of his liver and yanked it out, then began munching on it like it was caviar.

Wilson turned and threw up, followed by Mary Jane, who splattered her breakfast across the counter, bits of undigested apple-sausage spreading across the Formica.

Pastor James, munching on his own liver, turned around, and upon seeing Beth again, dropped the liver and moved towards her.

Another shot rang out and a small hole appeared on Pastor James forehead, a larger hole appearing out the back. The head was rocked to the side, but he didn't go down. He turned to stare at Bubba, who was still holding his .38 in a shaking hand, and snarled.

"What the hell? I shot him in the head, for Christ sakes! That's supposed to work, right?" He turned to DJ, a few feet to his right. "I mean, that's what you do to zombies, right? You shoot 'em in the head!"

DJ shrugged. "Guess he's not a horror buff, maybe he didn't get the memo."

Bubba's mouth was hanging open like he was the biggest dullard on the planet.

Ignoring him, DJ turned to Pastor James again, who was already trying to get at Beth and Jake. Jake had pushed a trash barrel in front of him and Beth and the barrel was only thing stopping Pastor James from reaching them. While Pastor James tried to get to them, pieces of his organs slid out of his gaping chest wound to splatter onto the floor, the sound reminiscent of wet spaghetti dropped from a six foot height.

"Come on, DJ, do something, man!" Jake yelled, pushing and pulling the barrel.

"All right, then, enough of this shit. Jake, get back and cover your eyes, you too Beth!" He screamed, then crossed the distance separating him from Pastor James, and when he was no more than a foot away, he leveled the shotgun at the man's head and fired his second shot.

Pastor James snarling head disappeared in a brilliant pink cloud of blood, bone matter and brains. The booth behind the man was bathed in gore, bits of scalp splattering against the glass wall of the diner to then slowly slide downward, leaving small snail trails of scarlet and gray matter. A larger vapor cloud lingered in the air, the sweet smell of death permeating the diner.

The decapitated body seemed to waver for a moment, then it turned and stumbled away, hands reaching out to guide it like a blind man. No one spoke, all staring at the headless corpse as it bumped into booths and knocked over glassware on the nearby counter.

"Jesus, H. Christ, he's still not dead!" Bubba screamed, aiming his .38 at the headless corpse, but not firing.

With a scowl of annoyance, DJ moved to the headless body, calling out to Jake at the same time.

"Jake, give me a hand with this asshole, will ya?"

Jake did as he was told, hesitantly crossing the diner and grabbing Pastor James flailing right arm. DJ did the same with the left and the two men trapped the body between them.

"What do we do with him?" Jake asked, his face filled with disgust. Blood pumped from the neck to spill onto the floor, making the linoleum slippery.

"Let's bring him to the walk-in. We can toss him in there for now," DJ told him.

With a curt nod, Jake helped DJ push and carry Pastor James decapitated body to the rear of the diner, and the large, walk-in refrigerator. When they had reached their destination, DJ opened the latch, cold air spilling out to fog the air. With a heave, they pushed the body into the walk-in and slammed the door. Immediately a pounding could be heard, flesh banging on the cold stainless steel door.

Jake turned to DJ, his eyes wide with shock. "DJ, man, what the hell is going on around here? How the fuck did that guy keep going like that?"

DJ shrugged. "It's like I said, Jake, zombies are here. I knew it wouldn't stop with the animals."

"That's ridiculous. There's no such thing as zombies, you are so full of shit."

"Oh yeah? Then how do you explain that?" DJ asked and pointed to the walk-in door. The pounding continued, as if to illustrate his point.

"I can't, dammit. But there's got to be a rational…"

He was cut off by another scream from the front of the diner, followed by angry yells and frightened shouts. Mary Jane's voice was heard at the top of the scale, her scream long and high.

"What the…? Oh Christ, what now?" DJ muttered and the two men took off, leaving the headless body trapped in the walk-in. He had a vision of the glass doors shattered, the hundreds of dead animals streaming into his diner to attack his friends and the patrons alike.

Upon reaching the main floor of the diner, DJ and Jake stopped short, both shocked at the visceral scene in front of them.

Wilbur had returned from the bathrooms, only he wasn't really Wilbur anymore. The man had been unable to staunch the flow of blood from his severed digits and had bled out on the bathroom floor. After expelling his last breath, eyes closed, they had promptly snapped open, but where there was once a light that said Wilbur was home, that bulb was shattered, never to be turned on again.

And now Wilbur was lying on top of Mary Jane, his face digging into her neck. Mary Jane was screaming, her blood spraying up to the ceiling, her carotid artery shooting red plasma across the counter.

Wilson, Bubba and Carlos, were on top of Wilbur, trying to get the man to let the woman go, but Wilbur was a big man and now he didn't feel pain. Carlos was punching Wilbur in the side of his torso, but was receiving no reaction for his troubles. Beneath him, Mary Jane's legs kicked and swung around as she bled out on the counter she had painstakingly cleaned only an hour ago.

Finally it was Bubba who did what had to be done. With the .38 in his hand, he placed the muzzle against Wilbur's left ear and fired, sending the man's brains out the opposite ear. The head rocked and the smell of gunpowder filled the already foul air of the diner, but Wilbur didn't stop. His head snapped back and he began feeding again, oblivious to the large hole in his head. Bubba was able to lean over and peer through the hole, seeing DJ and Jake on the other side as the two man ran towards them to help.

Then DJ and Jake joined the melee and they managed to pry Wilbur off the beleaguered woman.

"What do we do with him, DJ? The son of a bitch won't go down!" Bubba screamed. Carlos replied in Spanish, his words jumbled together.

DJ had Wilbur's left arm behind him, and with the hold on good, Wilbur couldn't get at him. Though Wilbur was a big man, DJ was bigger.

"Come on, we'll shove him in the walk-in with the other one," he gasped, and as one, all the men pushed Wilbur to the back of the diner and the waiting walk-in.

This time it was harder. Wilbur kept trying to bite everyone, teeth clacking like a dentist's toy chompers. Jake almost lost a finger and Carlos almost lost a piece of his right cheek, but soon they were at the walk-in again.

"Jake, get it open, will ya?" DJ called.

Jake did so, and the instant he opened the walk-in, concentrating on Wilbur, the headless body of Pastor James jumped out, pushed him aside and ran back down the hall and into the diner.

"Oh for the love of…Jake, go get that bastard, we've got this one!" DJ screamed as the men managed to shove Wilbur inside the walk-in. Jake took off after the headless corpse, which was bouncing off the walls and spinning in circles, hands out in front of it as it tried to find its way.

DJ, with the help of the others, shoved Wilbur into the walk-in, and when he was sure Carlos and Bubba had him, he let go.

"Hold him, boys, I need to do something or every time we open the door one of these bastards is gonna get loose."

He reached up to the top shelf where some twine for wrapping roasts was sitting. Pulling the small roll down, he quickly tied Wilbur's hands together and then secured them to a larger shelf mounted to the wall.

"Okay, boys, let him go. He's not going anywhere."

They let go and took a step back, the men staring at what was once Wilbur, but was now something else. The dead trucker snarled, teeth gnashing, blood dripping from his chin to splatter on the floor. His eyes rolled in his head and his breath came in gasps, clouding in front of his face from the cold. Everyone was so shocked by what was happening, no one thought to question why the man was breathing at all. The hole in his head dripped brain matter and every time Wilbur turned his head, the coleslaw on the shelf behind him could be seen clearly.

"He's loco," Carlos said in a low voice.

"The man's right, DJ," Bubba said. "That ain't Wilbur no more. What the hell happened to him?"

No one spoke then as each man stared at Wilbur. Every time the dead trucker turned his head, the large hole in his skull would reflect the wan light coming in from the hallway. Bits of brain fell out to fall onto the tiles of the walk-in.

DJ shook his head, realizing how absolutely ludicrous the situation was.

"This is some shit we're in, here, boys, I'll tell you that. Some real and true end of the world shit. I'm talking the four horsemen kind of stuff." His breath fogged in front of him due to the cold temperature in the walk-in.

A thump from outside in the hall had DJ looking up and swinging his head out the door to see what was happening. He turned to see Jake kicking and pushing Pastor James headless corpse back towards the walk-in.

"Little help?" Jake called out.

Pastor James slipped and fell heavily to the floor, more of his internal organs falling out. His heart bounced twice and then slid away like a hockey puck, the Pastor reaching out with his hand to try and catch it. But with no head, he missed, the heart bouncing away. With a sigh and roll of his eyes, Jake pulled the headless body to its feet again.

The men exited the walk-in and easily shoved Pastor James back inside the cooler, the body falling over onto Wilbur. The two zombies became entangled and that was the last view they had until DJ closed the door again, sliding the padlock through the latch just in case.

"Well, at least they have each other," Jake said with a wry grin. Truth was, he was scared shitless and only cracked jokes to cover his nervousness.

"Yeah, I guess there's that," DJ said. "Come on; let's see how Mary Jane is doing."

The men jogged down the hallway single file and were soon back in the diner.

Mary Jane was still on the counter, a few people hovering over her. Matt and Liz, the young married couple, were trying to stop the blood but it was hard, the neck wound not allowing them to apply pressure. Beth was holding the wounded woman's hand, not knowing what to do and Mary Jane's breathing was coming in dry rasps. You didn't have to be a doctor to know she was mortally wounded.

DJ went to her and held her free hand, gazing down at her.

"Hey there, girl, you all right?"

Mary Jane tried to smile, but it didn't come. She was woozy and it was hard to focus.

"DJ, am I gonna turn into something like Wilbur or that other man? I don't want to do that, DJ. When a person dies, they're supposed to stay dead. I want to go to Heaven, DJ. How can I if I'm still walking around?"

Big, tough, hardass, DJ, wiped a tear from his eye.

"I don't know, honey, I really don't. But if things go the way they have, then yeah, you're gonna come back. Unless…"

"Oh, no fuckin' way, DJ. No way man. It's Mary Jane here. You can't!" Jake screamed, already knowing what DJ was suggesting. It was obvious to anyone in the room what was going to happen to the hapless waitress.

DJ turned to glare at Jake, eyes wide with anger and loss. "Yeah, Jake, I fucking can! This is my diner, goddammit, and don't any of you assholes forget that!" Then his countenance softened and he gazed back down at Mary Jane, whose eyes were fluttering. "She's my friend. And has been for a long time. Hell, we opened this place together. I remember when she walked in here with a big smile and the flyer I'd sent out to some of the other nearby stores in Atkinson. She wanted a job. *Just passing through,* she'd said. Back then this place was stilled called Beekman's Diner. And here it is, ten years later and she's still here." He turned to look at Jake again. "So yeah, I can do it if she wants me to."

He looked down at Mary Jane's pain filled face and nodded. "Yeah, I can do it, 'cause I have to."

"I want you to, DJ. Don't let me end up like one those people." She coughed then, blood shooting from her mouth to coat her chin and blend in with her blood-soaked neck.

With a heavy sigh, DJ slung his shotgun over his shoulder and pushed Liz out of the way, the neck wound seeping more now that she wasn't attempting to apply pressure. DJ scooped the woman up on his arms and carried her to the back of the diner, to his office. Jake moved in his way and stopped him halfway there and looked up into his tall boss' eyes.

"DJ, man, there's got to be another way. Maybe we can get her to a hospital."

DJ shook his head. "No, Jake, we both know it's too late for that. Now get out of my way and let me honor her last wish." The two men stared at each other for three heartbeats and then Jake nodded and moved out of the way. His hands were molded into tight fists and his jaw was taught. He hated this, but he too, knew it was what had to be.

DJ disappeared into the rear hallway, and a second later, Jake heard his office door open and then close, the thud much more final than usual when the man went to his office. Beth moved next to Jake and they wrapped their arms around one another. Matt and Liz were standing near the counter, both holding hands. Bubba and Wilson stood side by side, Bubba fingering his .38. Carlos was alone near the kitchen door, a rag in his hand, one he couldn't let go as he wrung it again and again. The small man with the bird book, who had never left his booth, now looked up, his knuckles whiter as he squeezed the binding of his book held tight against his chest. The small woman with the brown hair moved closer to the corner of her booth, trying to look as small as possible.

No one spoke, no one moved. With the exception of the dead animals banging on the glass doors, the diner was silent.

Then one shotgun blast, muffled behind a closed door, rebounded off the walls and everyone knew the deed had been done.

DJ had kept his word; there was no more to be said.

6

More trouble

Birdman sees a bird

EIGHT MINUTES HAD passed since the shotgun blast had rung out and Jake was the first to regain his mobility. The others stayed rooted to their spots, all still feeling the weight of yet another death of one of their slowly shrinking group of survivors.

Wanting to check on what was happening in the parking lot, Jake took Beth's hand and led her to the door.

"Come on, I want to make sure it's okay out there."

She nodded and followed him, leaving the others to mourn the loss of Mary Jane. DJ was still in his office, what he was doing in there was anyone's guess.

Upon reaching the glass doors, Jake opened the blinds and gazed down at the dead animals clawing at the doors. Possums, beavers, rats, lemmings, deer, mice, a few housecats and three stray and very dead dogs all tried to gain entry. Some had no eyes, others no jaws, some were nothing but bone and fur and Jake shook his head, still not believing what he was witnessing.

"What do you think is making them keep going?" Beth asked as she stared at what was once a cute bunny rabbit, but now looked like something out of a nightmare.

Jake shook his head, his eyes jumping from animal to animal.

"No idea, but whatever it is, I hope it stops. Shit, Beth, we could be trapped in here forever."

"What? That's crazy," she scoffed. "Surely the army or something will regain order, I mean how bad could it be?"

Jake began counting on his fingers. "How bad? Let's see, how many dead animals are there in New Hampshire? Or better yet, the world? Shit, Beth, we may be so screwed we can't even imagine it yet."

"Well, I hope you're wrong, because if you aren't, I don't want to think about it."

"Yeah, I know what you mean," he said as he looked out onto the parking lot. It was then he spotted movement near the cars at the front of the door. At first he could only see two pairs of shredded feet, but as each second passed, he saw two forms rise to a standing position. His voice caught in his throat and he began to make a small mewling sound as he stared at the two abominations slowly walking around the front of the cars and moving towards the diner. Beth saw them too, at almost the exact same time, and her breath lodged in her throat.

"Oh my God, it can't be" she said as she stared through the glass doors, her heart pumping fast in terror.

But it was.

Ruth and Walter had slept long enough and now they were back, only now they were playing for the other side.

The married couple had lost some weight since they had left the diner. Both of their anatomies were nothing but bloodied bones and pieces of gristle. All their skin was stripped from their bodies, leaving them looking like one of those anatomy exhibits in the Museum of Science in Boston, where the human body is exposed, all the tendons and muscles on display.

When they walked, tendons could be seen flexing, and bones shifted in their sockets. Small pieces of flesh and gore slid from their bones to fall onto the pavement. No sooner did the gobbets of meat fall, then some smaller rodent would scoop it up, and then quickly scurry back under the car from whence it came.

Inside the hollow cavities of the two mobile skeletons, pygmy shrews, salamanders, chipmunks and a few deer mice all scavenged for remaining flesh, their rotten teeth chewing and gnawing on the flayed bones.

The two bodies slowly moved across the parking lot, their bones glistening in the noonday sun. There was no true way to describe what Jake was seeing, but deep down he knew it was a horror that would never leave him.

The headless deer wandered in front of the skeletons and the animals were pushed out of the way, the deer heading off towards the highway.

Walter was the first in line, and he swiveled his head, his spine moving slightly with his movements. He was missing his left eye, but his right was fine, only a pink and white orb, minus the eyelid. The orb shifted in its socket as Walter searched his surroundings, then he moved to the glass doors. Some of the animals parted for the two walking, red skeletons, and slowly, one foot at a time, the dead couple made their way to the diner's doors. The three steps that led to the doors was slightly more difficult for the skeletons to manage and Jake watched as knee joints flexed and moved, the two corpses slowly moving up the steps.

But if that wasn't bad enough, the next thing to happen totally threw Jake for a loop.

Walter climbed the stairs, and when he was standing in front of the glass doors, he held up his right hand, now nothing but bones and red gristle. Behind Jake, the others had seen what was happening and slowly were moving to stand behind Jake and Beth.

Meanwhile, Walters' lone orb stared at Jake, the man and the skeleton locking gazes. Walter took his right index finger, stuck it onto his chest cavity to get it good and bloody, and then touched it to the glass. He wrote slowly, his finger like a pen and it took Jake a second to understand what the skeleton was writing. Then his mind put it all together and he read it aloud.

"Let us in or you will suffer more," he read out loud.

Walter's eyes watched Jake speak and he nodded, the skull moving up and down slowly. The jaws opened wide and the tongue-less mouth hissed, but with no lungs anymore the gesture was silent. Then a sludge-like rat popped out of the mouth, a juicy tidbit in its jaws and hopped out to scurry away.

"Jake, did that skeleton just do what I think it did?" Beth asked in shock.

"Yeah, Beth, it did, as hard as that is to believe."

Bubba pushed past Jake and stuck his finger at the glass, as if he could push Walter away with it.

"You can go fuck yourself, you dead fuck. If you come in here, I will blow you the fuck away! You got that?"

"Uh, Bubba. I don't think he can hear you. For one thing the glass is pretty thick and the second is Walter there doesn't have any ears left. Probably no eardrums either. In fact, I don't even know if that *is* Walter. For all I know that's Ruth there looking at us."

"Aww no, he can hear me, the dead bastard. 'Sides, the taller one is Walter, got to be." He turned back to Walter and Ruth. "Lie down and die, for Christ's sakes, you're dead!"

"I don't think they're gonna oblige you, Bubba," Wilson said from behind him.

Bubba turned suddenly, glad to now have a real live person to vent his rage on.

"Don't tell me what they can and can't do, you hear me? Get the hell out of the way, dammit, I need a beer." Bubba pushed his way through the small crowd of patrons, muttering about the insanity of walking skeletons and dead animals.

Carlos moved next to Jake and made the sign of the cross, then finished by kissing the St. Anthony medal on his chest.

"El morte," he said in a whisper. "Impossible?"

Jake turned to Carlos, a frown on his lips.

"Maybe so, Carlos, but my eyes say different."

"Si, si," Carlos said and moved away, muttering prayers in Spanish under his breath.

Beth took his hand and squeezed hard while her eyes stared at Ruth. The woman was on the best diet in the world and had dropped all her body weight in minutes. Only now she was one of the walking dead and wasn't about to go clubbing with her slim new figure.

"I'm scared, Jake," she said. "How the hell are we supposed to deal with this? I mean, God, there are walking skeletons outside the diner. As if the animals weren't bad enough. And then there's the Pastor running around without a head and the other guy, the trucker, and then the waitress dies." She shook her head. "It's all so unbelievable. I keep thinking I'm gonna wake up and be in my sister's bed in Maine and all of this will have just been a bad dream."

"Yeah, Beth, I know what you mean, and you know what? I'm not afraid to say that I'm scared, too. But whatever's happening is happening and I'll be damned if I'm gonna let it kill me, too." He gave her a slight smirk, pulling her hand gently towards the counter, where Liz had cleaned up most of Mary Jane's blood. The woman had wanted to do it, feeling good about having a small chore to accomplish, a small way of controlling what was happening in her spiraling life.

"Come on, let's get something to drink and try to forget about all this shit. We're safe in here for the time being. They can't get in." Jake turned away from the doors, but before he did, he pulled down the shades on the glass doors again. The two skeletons, dripping blood onto the landing, opened their jaws wide, then they were lost from sight. It was Jake that caught the image of Walter as the shades went down. He might have been wrong, but he could have sworn Walter was flipping him off, his bony middle finger upraised in the international salute.

Deciding he was seeing things, I mean, it was one thing to want to kill him, but to flip him off? Now that was just downright ridiculous.

With the shades closed, Jake turned to the people behind him, ushering them away from the doors.

"Come on, folks, the shows over. Let's see about getting some food, I'm starving." He really wasn't hungry, but he knew he needed to say that to get everyone moving.

Slowly at first, but then a little faster, everyone moved away from the doors. Liz had already begun setting up soft drinks on the counter after hearing Jake's comment. She was taking Mary Jane's place. The ledger with the lists of who was taking what was forgotten, Liz having already tossed the notepad under the counter.

She didn't think DJ would mind and if he did, she didn't care.

*   *   *

The entire time the incident with the skeleton occurred, the small man with the bird book sat silently, staring out the windows. There were so many kinds of birds out there. Sure, they were all dead, but still, some he thought he would never have been lucky enough to see in his lifetime and as he watched them hop around, he realized he was seeing the find of the century, or at least in his small life.

Plus, thinking about the birds helped him to stay focused and not go crazy. He was a panicky man in the best of times and with dead animals and zombies in the diner, to say he was on the edge would be an understatement.

Then he saw something he thought he would never see; a rare specimen of peregrine Falcon. A Falco peregrinus to be exact. The bird was becoming scarce in New York and he didn't have the money to travel all over the states searching for one. New Hampshire was the best he could afford. And here one was. It was definitely dead, the left side of its head was caved in and one wing looked to be hanging on by threads of muscle, but there it was, his Holy Grail of birds in his bird watching club. Opening his book, he skimmed through the pages until he found the one he wanted.

"Oh my, it is beautiful, isn't it," he said to himself.

He picked up his digital camera and zoomed in on the bird, and then the others surrounding it, snapping pictures again and again. He simply could not get enough of them. The falcon seemed to look at him, cocking its head to the side. The small man paid no mind that the bird had a bloody eyeball in its beak, the ocular fluid dripping from the stringy veins to drip onto the ground.

"Oh my, what a beautiful specimen," he said again, totally oblivious to the other people around him. This was what he lived for and this was why he had come here.

Lost in a world of bird watching, he snapped picture after picture, in perfect bliss.

7

A QUIET MOMENT

NIGHT WAS FALLING upon the diner, and inside, the patrons tried to get comfortable. Matt and Liz were curled up in a booth, Matt's hands hidden under the table, lost in the shadows. Every now and then Liz would giggle, the two having a little fun to let off some stress. Across the diner, Bubba and Wilson sat with a half dozen bottles of beer on the table between them. The two were good and buzzed, the .38 sitting on the table next to Bubba's right hand. Carlos was seated at the counter, the remains of a sandwich lying half eaten on a plate. He was looking down at the St. Anthony medal on his chest, twisting the medallion back and forth as he thought of his family. The small woman with the brown hair was dozing, her hands twitching like she was dog caught in a fitful dream.

Birdman was still watching the dead animals through the diner's glass window. He had stopped taking pictures with the fall of night, but his eyes were wide with manic glee. Every hour that passed showed him yet another new species of bird, some even rarer than the Falco peregrinus was. His eyes darted back and forth as he looked to the next sighting. The fact that every avian was dead meant nothing to him, and the right side of his mouth began curving up in a slight tick, the twitching lip dancing each time he chuckled. He was slowly falling into madness, his psyche fragile on the best of days certainly wasn't up to the task of coping with his new surroundings. But for now he was content to watch the birds as they fought over pieces of bloody flesh in the pale moonlight. He barely paid attention to the two blood-red skeletons walking around the parking lot like something out of a Halloween movie. One time, as the skeletons crossed the parking lot, Walter paused and turned his skeletal frame to the diner. Seeing Birdman watching him, he crossed his left arm with his right; pointing the right hand straight up into the air and giving Birdman the international sign for *fuck you.*

Birdman never noticed, too wrapped up in the Purple Martin that was hopping onto the roof of a car behind the animated skeleton. Walter decided he was wasting his time and moved away; Ruth following him like the dutiful wife. It seemed the two were getting along better in death than they ever had in life.

DJ was nowhere to be seen. Since the shotgun blast had gone off, ending Mary Jane's suffering, the large owner of the diner had not come out of his office. Jake had knocked once and had received a curt rebuff. So, with at least knowing the man was still alive, he'd left him alone to his solitude. The other patrons had followed his lead, too, and had stayed away after Jake had filled them in.

Now, in the back room of the diner, where Pastor James had been laid down to rest before he had attacked Wilbur, Jake and Beth lay entwined in each others arms, the surrounding shadows covering their bodies. There were fresh sheets on the cot, the old ones tossed in the trash. Their bare feet were rubbing together and it was obvious that the two were naked under the bedclothes. Beth's face was covered in sweat, her breathing coming in gasps as she orgasmed for the second time. A small cassette radio sat on the floor, AC/DC playing softly, the words *ride on* drifting from the tiny speaker.

Rolling away from Jake, and almost falling off the cot, she let out a sigh, her blushing face a deep red.

"Wow, that was intense. I'll tell you this, Jake; you sure know how to do it like a champ."

Jake sucked in a breath of his own, his ego pumped up from her compliment.

"Well, thanks, Beth, I wish I could say I was good 'cause I've had a lot of practice, but I guess I make up in enthusiasm for what I lack in experience."

She chuckled, wiping her face with the end of the sheet.

"I'll second that, and don't apologize for not having screwed a hundred women before me. Trust me; no woman wants to hear that."

"Not a problem then," he grinned and reached out with his arm for her to scoot closer to him. "Out here in the boonies, it's not as easy as you might think to get a date. And I've never been one to go in for the bar scene."

Beth nodded and curled up closer to him, their flesh sticking together from the sweat covering their naked bodies. Neither minded, enjoying the closeness of one another.

An hour ago the two had gone to the back room so he could give her a change of clothing. She had been covered in blood from when the deer had been shot in front of her and then again when Pastor James and Wilbur had been shot, and there had been no time for her to do anything but use a few napkins to try and clean her face and arms. So when things were as calm as they were going to get, he'd led her to the back room where he kept a few things in case of an emergency, such as covering himself with grease when he changed the fryer on Sundays.

One thing had led to another, both of them needing someone to lean on, and they had fallen into a soft kiss, which soon became much more. The first time they made love had been awkward, neither wanting to act like they weren't in control, but after the first orgasm and they had a chance to relax, to talk for some time, the second time had been much easier, more relaxed. And Jake knew the third time was going to be even better, he just needed a few minutes to recharge his batteries.

The sheet slipped down a bit and his gaze drifted to Beth's small, but pert breasts, the nipples hard and pointy. He leaned over and kissed the right one with his lips, causing her to giggle and squirm away.

"Stop that, you horndog, haven't you had enough yet?"

He shook his head, his lips rubbing the nipple as he did it. "No way, babe, I haven't even gotten started yet. I don't know about you, but I've got some much needed time to make up for."

She pushed his head away and moved up tight against him, their sweaty bodies sticking together yet again. With her soft, warm body so close, he could already feel himself rising to the occasion for round three.

Beth turned her head slightly and gazed out the only window, the window was tiny, and head high in the small room, and she could see the dark sky, but with the moonlight, the sky took on an otherworldly color, the yellow color still visible even with night having fallen. In fact, now, with night fully descended, the sky seemed to glow, the amber waves shimmering back and forth as if they had a mind of their own.

"You know, I think whatever's happening has something do with that comet. I mean, we're in its tail right? And all this stuff happened at the same time."

"Yeah, I guess you could be right about that," Jake said. "Why, what's your point?"

She turned to him and slapped him playfully on the cheek, not hard, just a love tap. "My point, you sexy man, is that if it is the comet, then all we have to do is stay alive for two more days. When the comet leaves, maybe all this craziness will be over."

Jake lowered his eyebrows as he considered her words.

"Yeah, that's a good point. So all we need to do is just hang out here for two more days and then we'll be okay." He frowned. "But wait. What if you're wrong?"

"Hmm, yeah, what if I'm wrong." She creased her eyes and wrinkled her nose as she thought that one over.

"Well, then I guess we'll have to make a run for it. You have a car right?"

"Sure, but it's parked across the lot. DJ makes all the employees park at the end so the customers can get the good parking. Of course, he always parks his car right at the door."

Beth nodded. "Good, then if we need to run for it, we'll just have to take DJ's car."

Jake shrugged, the gesture barely noticed under the sheets.

"Sure, I guess we could do that."

She smiled then and before Jake could stop her, she climbed on top of him, the sheet rolling off her smooth skin. Looking down on him, she grinned mischievously.

"Well, now that we've settled that, want to take another trip around the world?"

Jake answered by pulling her off him and then climbing on top of her, the maneuver almost tossing them both to the floor, the unstable cot not able to handle their actions.

"Sure, but I'll drive, babe."

She stretched out her arms and grinned seductively up at him.

"Works for me, handsome, just make sure you keep the car in its lane and I'll be very happy."

He rolled his eyes and smirked. "Oh, please, enough with the metaphors." Then he leaned down and the two kissed, which in seconds became much, much more.

With the sky above the diner glowing with an amber hue, the two lovers joined together for the third time.

8

THE BEGINNING OF THE END

THE NEXT MORNING had Carlos making breakfast for everyone. Though the power was out, the gas was still on and Carlos boiled some eggs and fried up some sausages. Everyone ate something, though no one was really hungry. It had been a hard night with the constant banging, scraping and tapping of the undead animals attacking the glass of the diner. But they couldn't gain entry and all were hopeful they would survive their ordeal.

Beth and Jake had filled the others in on Beth's idea that once the comet left Earth, the animals would die. Some agreed, while others didn't.

"What if whatever has started all this shit is still here?" Bubba asked while wolfing down a plate full of hardboiled eggs. "What if nothing changes?"

Beth shrugged, not having an answer for him and it was Jake who replied for her.

"Then I guess we're pretty well screwed, don't ya think?"

Bubba frowned, not liking the answer but knowing it was the truth.

The morning passed with each of them trying to stay busy. Bubba had produced a deck of cards from his shirt pocket and Matt, Liz, Bubba, and Wilson played poker. They wanted Jake to make the fifth player but he declined. His eyes kept returning to the windows where Walter and Ruth could be seen moving about. Walter saw Jake watching him and the skeleton flipped him off, the bony and bloody index finger aimed high, his jaw opened wide, the gaping hole where a tongue should be staring back. Jake turned away, not wanting to look anymore. Every time he looked at the two skeletons he felt sick. Beth had taken it better than him, as if the walking dead was no big deal, but last night, while she thought he was asleep, he had heard her sobbing. She was a strong woman, but she was as human as the rest of them. Jake wondered how his folks were and his sister. Were they okay? Or had they been killed. He tried not to think about them too much as there was nothing he could do for them at the moment.

No, for the time being he needed to worry about himself, and Beth, too. After last night, the two had grown close, and their morning lovemaking session had only brought them closer. Jake had never thought he would find someone like Beth. She was beautiful, smart, strong and tough. Everything he had ever wanted in a woman; all rolled into one. He couldn't help but wonder how if the animals hadn't come back to life, would he have ever met her. Probably not.

She wouldn't have even come to the diner, but would have continued on to Maine, never knowing he existed. He turned slightly and watched her without her seeing him. She was talking with Matt and Liz. The two were a nice couple and were as scared as the rest of them.

Jake's gaze flicked to the rear hall, where DJ's office was located. The large man still hadn't made an appearance, but when Jake had gone to the door earlier, he had heard the distinct sound of the man snoring. He was still in there and Jake could only imagine what was going on in there.

His attention turned to the back of the diner, and the rear hallway which led to where the walk-in was. The sound of banging could be heard, the two zombies trying to get out. They were safely ensconced. The walk-in was made of stainless steel and the padlock was on the latch. No, at least those two wouldn't be causing any more trouble. He wondered about Mary Jane. Was her body still in the office with DJ? Or had the man taken her out of the office in the middle of the night and placed her in the walk-in with the others. It was doubtful, as the instant the door would have been opened, the headless body of Pastor James would have tried to escape .

In the end, it didn't really matter. Deciding he would join Beth, Liz and Matt, he picked up an apple from the fruit bowl Carlos had placed on the main counter, nodded to the dishwasher, and then went over to the others.

Meanwhile, Birdman was staring out the window, his attention fascinated by the rare and endangered birds he was seeing. Once again, all the birds were dead, some only feathers and bones, but he didn't care. He had already used up one flash card in his camera and was now on his second one. He was writing the sightings down in his notebook, checking off the ones he'd found in his bird book, too. He was in Heaven. If it wasn't for the birds, he would have gone mad long before, when the outbreak had first started.

Watching through his camera, he mumbled to himself.

"Oh my, what a beautiful specimen of Charadrius melodus. Oh, and will you look at that? A perfect Cistothorus platensis. I must document that one. Oh, and that is a marvelous Sterna paradisaea." He quickly snapped pictures and then wrote them down, his hunger for the next bird spotting growing inside him. He was becoming more and more unstable, sweat beading on his forehead and dripping into his eyes. His heart was beating fast and his breath was coming in gasps. Off in the corner booth, no one noticed him. He was like the party guest who blended with the wallpaper, always there, but no one would remember him.

"Oh, will you look at that. A Podilymbus podiceps, excellent." And then he saw the one that blew him away. The one species he thought he would never see in his lifetime.

"I don't believe it," he said to himself. "A Pandion haliaetus, and in perfect condition." He tried to take its picture, but the bird hopped away and went behind a car.

"Oh, no, you can't get away from me, not after so long. I've waited so long to find you!" He jumped up from his booth, camera in one hand and book in the other, and then dashed across the diner. At first, no one noticed him, too caught up in what they were doing. But as Birdman approached the glass doors to the diner, Jake looked up, realizing the man wasn't slowing down. In fact, he was picking up speed as he approached the secured doors.

"Hey, buddy, where do you think you're going?" Jake called out, but the man ignored him. Jake realized only seconds before Birdman reached the glass doors what was going to happen, though he couldn't believe anyone would be so stupid as to do it.

Birdman had eyes only for the endangered bird in the parking lot and he barely noticed the dead animals scratching at the doors. Before anyone could stop him, he pushed on the doors, throwing them wide open, and began stepping out onto the landing and the parking lot beyond. But he never got that far. No sooner did he open the doors than he was overwhelmed by dead animals. Deer, cats, rats, possum, rabbits, mice, salamanders, a few Black bears. Not to mention coyotes, foxes and a few stray dogs, were only a few of the dead species to swarm into the diner among the hundreds of different rodent species.

Birdman had time for one screech and then he was knocked to the floor, his body pitching backward, the camera going in one direction, his bird book in the other. He managed the one shriek and then a rat jumped into his mouth, closing off his cries. The dead animal clawed and scraped at his lips, teeth digging into his flesh and tearing it apart as it burrowed into his body. While that was happening, his torso was sliced apart by razor sharp claws, his intestines pulled from his abdomen, where they were strung out and became wrapped around the legs and hooves of the other animals. His innards were yanked out like a magician's handkerchief trick, yard after bloody yard of greasy, blood-red rope falling out onto the floor of the diner. But by then the Birdman was dead, spared the suffering he would have endured if not for a quick slice to his neck by sharp talons, severing his jugular; his blood shooting out to splatter on his precious bird book, staining the pages crimson.

Jake jumped up, seeing the animals swarming into the diner.

"Holy shit, what the hell did that idiot do?" Jake screamed, pulling Beth towards him.

No one answered him, everyone in shock for the precious seconds that were sorely needed to protect themselves. Then Bubba aimed his gun at the first few animals and fired off a few rounds.

"Who cares, Jake, they're inside, now fight dammit or we're all dead!"

Jake snapped out of his stupor and tossed a few tables and chairs into the center aisle, causing the animals to detour around them. Wilson was caught entirely off guard and he was overwhelmed in seconds, brought to the diner's floor with barely a whimper. A bear and a deer, along with a large moose, had knocked him down and were chewing at his skin and limbs like he was a Thanksgiving Day feast for the homeless. One animal got his left arm in its jaws and another got his right arm and they pulled, the limbs peeling off the man like he was being drawn and quartered, and the sound of tearing flesh filled the diner, sounding strangely like someone was peeling a large orange.

Blood spread out on the floor, pints of red plasma coating the tiles with crimson, the animals lapping it up greedily.

Carlos saw Wilson go down and before he thought it through, he tried to save his fellow survivor. But his attempt was doomed to failure. Just as Carlos reached the bifurcated man, a badger lunged at his stomach, knocking him onto a table, the two crashing to the floor. Carlos' face hit the floor hard, blood coating his cheeks and chin. Spitting blood, he only had enough time to roll over and look down at his stomach before the badger flared its teeth and dove into his abdomen, its claws scratching like it was digging a hole in the ground.

Flesh gave way easily and the badger dove inside Carlos torso, the man tried to grab the tail, but slippery with blood, it slid through his hands like it was a greased pig.

The badger burrowed straight inside him and then turned and began moving upward. Carlos' body jerked and twitched and lumps on his flesh could be seen as the animal burrowed through organs and viscera. His clothing undulated with the movement and then a large lump appeared in his throat and he began spitting blood, his eyes so wide they looked like they were about to pop out of their sockets and bounce away.

Jake could only watch in horror as Carlos' neck exploded outward and the badger's head appeared, nose sniffing the air, its entire body bathed in scarlet.

Wiggling for a second, it hopped out and ran away, a chunk of the dishwasher's heart in its jaws. Carlos was dead, his arms spread out in front of him, his St. Anthony medal lying to the side, covered in blood. But no sooner did the badger leave, then the small rodent crew arrived to pick up the slack. Mice, rats and rabbits, to name a few, swarmed into the body cavity, the gaping wound resembling a burrow for the small animals. Carlos' body began to jerk again, as if the man was still alive, but that was just the rodents inside him as they ate their way through his body, some going all the way to his hands and feet before chewing their way to the surface.

It was their turn to feast and they were hungry.

Matt and Liz were stomping on any of the smaller animals and Bubba was keeping the larger ones at bay. But it was a losing battle. Though the bullets slowed the dead creatures, they quickly regained their balance and came at them again. Beth and Jake threw more tables and chairs in the way, trying to keep them at bay, but the blockade did nothing to stop the attacking dead birds, which flew at them, claws and beaks seeking tender flesh and exposed eyes. The only saving grace for the patrons was the birds couldn't fly well inside the diner, the low ceiling hindering their movements.

But they were still more than a match for the brown-haired woman who had said nothing since becoming trapped in the diner. With one soft scream, she was overwhelmed by animals. Some swarmed up her legs and began to devour her whole. Birds pecked out her eyes and claws sliced her flesh and the woman no one knew died a silent death in the booth she had hand-picked for a sandwich and coffee a day before. If only she had known then when she had picked that booth that a day later she would end up dying there, sitting in her own blood and bile, would she have picked another booth? Or would she have stayed there, accepting her fate in the world.

Then over the screeching, growling animals, Jake saw Walter and Ruth step into the diner. The blood was slightly dried on their bones, but both were still something incredible to behold. They reminded him of the movie *Jason and the Argonauts;* when Jason battled the living skeletons. Only he had no sword and no way of fighting the abominations. Walter turned to stare at him, his remaining eye squinting slightly. His jaw opened malevolently and he raised his right hand, index pointed at Jake and the others. A gargling sound issued from the gaping maw of a mouth and all the animals behind him swarmed into the diner. Hundreds of them poured through the open doorway, all wanting the tender meat now fighting for their last seconds on Earth.

"Oh my God, Jake, what do we do?" Beth screamed, pushing a possum away from her face, her hand coming back with tufts of rotting flesh and hair.

"I don't know, just keep fighting!"

The truth was, there was nothing else to do. Bubba fired his last round in the gun and then tried to reload, using the butt of the weapon as a makeshift club. The animals would give him no time to reload and he ended up just punching and kicking like the other survivors. Now the larger animals had nothing to stop them and they tried to climb over the table and chairs, their hooves and legs becoming tangled. But the simple amount of animals was more than enough to push the barricade to the side and Jake realized they had seconds before they would be overwhelmed. When he had a second, he reached out and pulled Beth to him.

He kissed her hard, tasting blood on her lips from some animals she had bitten or punched.

"I know I shouldn't say this, but I love you!"

Her eyes went wide.

"No, don't say anything. I know it sounds like horseshit, but I do. Even before we did it in the back room, I knew you were the girl for me. It just sucks we wont get to find out."

She shook her head and then she nodded, kissing him, too. Jake grinned; that was enough of an acknowledgment for him. Only seconds had passed and their time was over, the horde of animals, led by Walter and Ruth, storming the barricade, pushing the patrons against the far wall of the diner.

"Shit, I can't believe it's gonna end like this!" Bubba screamed, crushing a cat in his hands, the viscera squirting out the sides. He dropped the carcass to the ground and looked for his next target. There were plenty to choose from and he was ready to make them pay dearly

Liz screamed, a rat in her hair, and Matt reached up, yanked on its tail to dislodge it. The tail was pulled from the rotting rodent and the whip-like severed tail twitched back and forth in his hand like a garden snake. He tossed it away and reached up, slapping the rat from her head. Some of Liz's hair went with it, but she was safe for the moment. There was no time to say thank you, as three seagulls and a bald eagle dive bombed them, trying to claw out their eyes. Both ducked, but then found they were exposed to the jaws of two dogs and a baby deer, the latter having died weeks ago from exposure and hunger after being separated from its mother.

Feet stomped on the smaller animals like they were empty soda cans, internal organs and blood squirting out to coat the floor, making it slippery and treacherous, like an ice skating rink, and arms and legs kicked at the other attacking animals, but they all knew they had seconds to live. If only they had enough time to make their peace with death, but even that was to be denied them.

But just when they thought it was over, that all hope was lost and they were about to die, to be eaten alive by the swarm of dead creatures and then join the army in death, DJ's office door was kicked open and the large man stepped into the diner, slightly off to the side of the horde of animals. None noticed him; the patrons and animals caught up in their internal battle for dominance, but then Jake caught DJ out of the corner of his eye.

The man still wore his white Stetson hat, but other than that he was a changed man. He looked like a reject from a Rambo movie, decked out from head to toe with firearms and blades. A web belt hung across his chest and small orb-like shapes swung back and forth. Jake had seen enough war movies to recognize a grenade when he saw one. DJ's hands weren't empty either.

In his large hands was an M-60 machine gun, the large weapon looking like a toy as he cradled it in his arms. A massive, twelve-inch Bowie knife hung from a leather sheath at his side, the top and bottom of the blade serrated for maximum penetration and a jagged wound when removed from its victim.

If he had a bandanna on his head he would have looked like he'd just walked out of a Vietnam movie, but he quickly showed Jake and the dead animals the weapons weren't for show.

"Come and get some, you dead bastards! I got enough lead for everyone!" He laughed and screamed at the same time. Jake had heard rumors that DJ had a weapon's cellar, lined on both sides with purloined weapons. Some bought legally at gun shows, some in back alleyways in Boston and New York, but he had never believed the tales…until now.

DJ racked the machine gun, and with the ammunition draped over his arm like a scarf, he started spraying the animals closest to Jake and the others. Steel-jacketed rounds blew the animals' apart, gore and viscera spraying everywhere, some splattering the survivors. A moose tried for Bubba and before it could sink its teeth into the man's arm, twenty bullets smacked into its body, chewing it into shredded meat. The moose slowed and fell, but it was far from dead. With all four legs shattered it tried to use its chin to pull itself closer to Bubba to bite his leg. Bubba looked down, raised a large boot and stomped the head to the floor, brains seeping out of a busted cranium. He waved to DJ in thanks and then turned to see who he could help.

Matt and Liz were flailing their arms, trying to fend off the flying birds when Bubba picked up a chair and tossed it at the flock of birds. The sound of cracking wings and small bodies could be heard as the chair plummeted into them, then crashed to the floor.

DJ was howling like an insane man, the M-60 spitting death everywhere. The diner resembled Swiss cheese, holes everywhere. Almost all of the glass windows were shattered, and more animals were pouring inside, now not having to wait for the doorway to clear. The surrounding forest had been full of dead carcasses, thousands of them in different forms of decay. And now they were revived and they were hungry for meat.

Human meat.

When the animals near Jake and the others were relatively clear, DJ turned the smoking muzzle of the M-60 towards Walter. The skeleton had time for one open mouth gesture, and Jake found it amazing that he could see surprise registered on that fleshless skull, then DJ sent round after round at the dead man.

Bone was no match for bullets and Walter was blown to a thousand pieces, bone shards peppering the walls and ceiling. Ruth tried to run, to turn and escape through the door, but DJ stitched her from groin to neck, the bones shattering and fracturing. By the time he was finished only her head was still in the air, the rest of her having collapsed. Like gravity was on hold for one brief second, her red skull hovered in the air. Then more rounds went her way and the skull was pulverized, brain matter and bone splashing across the walls to slide down like someone had tossed a cherry pie against it.

But no sooner did DJ finish with the two skeletons then more animals came at him. The M-60 ran dry and he tossed it away, the hot barrel scorching a bunny rabbit when it landed on its carcass. The animal screeched and the smell of burnt meat could be detected, fried rabbit tantalizing all who smelled it.

Pulling two large handguns from shoulder holsters, DJ began firing, each round taking out another rotting animal, but there were hundreds of the creatures, and sooner or later he was going to exhaust his supply of ammunition.

Then the first animal got past his guard, a large vole sinking its teeth into his arm. He roared with anger and shot it away, shoving the muzzle of the handgun into its eye before firing. The animal exploded like a popped water balloon, the large caliber bullet simply destroying it, but there were many more behind it.

For the moment, all the animals were focused on the main danger in the room, as if they sensed DJ needed to be disposed of before they could deal with the other patrons.

"DJ, get out of there, there's too many!" Jake yelled. It was painfully obvious the man was becoming overwhelmed, only his white suit showing here and there under the pile of mottled fur.

"No shit. Don't you think I know that? Fuck it, Jake; it's too late for me. Get to the roof!" He yelled. "It's the only safe place."

Realizing his boss was right; Jake pulled Beth and punched Bubba on the arm to get the trucker's attention. Bubba let go of the squirrel in his hands, dropping the crushed carcass to the floor.

"Come on, DJ's right. The roof is our only option."

"But what about DJ?" Bubba asked and tossed a look over his shoulder. He got his answer a second later when he saw DJ's hands spread wide. The man was entirely covered with animals and it was only his massive strength and great girth that was allowing him to remain standing. In either hand was a grenade, thumbs in the pin rings.

"Oh shit, he's not gonna do that!" Bubba screamed, but he knew he was. "Go, Go! Move dammit! Move if you want to keep your ass in one piece!"

No one knew what he was hollering about but the tone of his voice was clear. Slipping and sliding on the floor, the remaining survivors crossed the diner, Jake in the lead. He reached the small door that led to the stairway to the roof, and after opening it, pushed Beth, Matt and Liz up it first. Bubba never hesitated, and before Jake could ask what was wrong with the trucker, Bubba picked him up and carried him into the stairwell like he was a child, pulling the door closed after him.

In the diner, DJ's face was a mess of torn flesh and blood. Both his eyes had been eaten away and mice and snakes crawled in his hair. His Stetson hat had fallen to the floor, the once pristine white hat now bathed in scarlet. It didn't matter, he couldn't see it anyway.

"See you in hell, you dead bastards! This is for Mary Jane!" He screamed and when his last word was uttered, a sparrow dove into his mouth, blocking off his airway. He coughed, in the darkness of his mind realizing he was dying, and then he felt talons across his stomach, his intestines slipping out to splatter onto the floor. The large Black bear sliced again and DJ bent at the knees, his mind filled with nothing but pain and agony.

Then he pulled the pins on the grenades with a flick of his thumbs, the two metal pins falling to the floor, the sound resembling two large cast iron skillets, the small tinkle seeming louder with the finality of what the two pins foretold. Was it his imagination that made him think that? Or was it his own anguish of knowing he had two seconds left to live.

He could feel the warm air on his exposed insides and he felt the slight tug as one of the animals yanked on a particularly juicy cord of intestine, then the grenades went off, and though he was blind, he could have sworn he saw a bright flash of light.

In an instant he was no more.

The shrapnel exploded outwards, slicing everything within twenty feet to mush. Every window still intact exploded outward and the walls of the diner buckled from the blast. Crystal shards blew out onto the dark parking lot, falling like hail, and the windshields of the closest cars were shattered and covered with blood and detritus. When the blast finally subsided, there was nothing left of DJ but his cowboy boots, the lower calves and feet still inside the boots, the muscle and tendons exposed where the blast had severed his legs. As for the animals, they were in disarray. More than half still mobile were headless and limbless. Many decapitated animals stumbled around, bumping into rubble and one another like blind mice. DJ's hat fluttered in the air and settled on the severed head of the Black bear, the animal rolling its eyes at the added apparel.

The sound of what seemed like rain, but was in fact all the bloody gobbets of meat, fell to the floor of the diner.

DJ's last stand had been a losing battle, there was no question of that, but he had done what he'd wanted and had taken more than three quarters of the dead animal horde with him into the afterlife.

Now the question was; would his sacrifice be enough to save the others until help arrived?

9

ENDINGS

J AKE WAS CARRIED up the roof stairs by Bubba like a sack of luggage, his head bouncing around like a rag doll, and when Bubba reached the access door, he charged onto the roof, dropping Jake without a warning and slamming the door hard, turning the small lock on the doorknob.

Gravel rose up to meet Jake's face and he turned his head at the last second, avoiding a nose full of small rocks. Rolling onto his side, he stared up at Beth's concerned face. Knowing there was no time for resting, he jumped to his feet, dizzy for a moment as he regained his equilibrium. Beth was looking past him, and he turned to see the edge of the diner, a small wall about three feet high which surrounded the edge of the roof. On this wall sat birds, dozens of them. And they were all dead. None of the birds moved, merely sat there, eyeing Jake and the others. To his left stood Bubba; his gun in his right hand, his red hair and beard seeming to glow in the moonlight. He was busily reloading it now that he had a chance. To his right stood Matt and Liz. They were holding hands and Jake saw Matt's other hand was balled into a fist. The man was ready to fight, and he would do what he had to do to save his wife.

Beth moved closer to Jake, so she could whisper her next question.

"What are they doing? They're just sitting there."

Jake slowly shook his head, having no idea what the killer birds were doing. There was a midnight-black crow in the middle, the others a few inches away from it, as if they were giving the black bird some space. The crow was filled with maggots, the small worms seeping out of the bird's beak and under its wings. Once again, Jake wondered how this bird could be moving, how it could exist at all.

Smoke rose from the opposite side of the wall, and Jake knew the grenades must have done some serious damage. They were all lucky the gas mains hadn't caught or the entire building would have gone up in a blazing inferno of fire and smoke, taking them all to Hell on a wild ride of death.

Taking a risk, nor knowing if movement would cause the birds to attack, Jake took two steps back and to the side and picked up a two-by-four lying on the roof. There were many odds and ends of debris scattered about; DJ too cheap to pay for rubbish disposal. With the makeshift wooden weapon in hand, he moved next to Beth again, then cast a furtive glance to Bubba, who had just finished reloading his gun. While he moved, the bird's shifted restlessly, but held their ground.

"How many bullets you got left for that thing?"

Bubba snuffed, then wiped his nose with the back of his free hand. "One more load and I'm empty. Reckon the bullets won't do much good against the birds, but if anything big tries to get at us, I'm ready."

As if to illustrate his point, the roof access door thumped in its frame. There was something on the other side and it wanted on the roof. The sounds of claws could be heard scraping the wood and Jake wondered how long the door would hold. It was nothing special, certainly not built for security.

Thinking of the door DJ had installed had him thinking of his former boss. In the end, the man had died valiantly, and had died trying to save them all, his sacrifice giving them the chance to escape. Though the man was an asshole, Jake would have never expected the man had some good inside him. Or perhaps DJ did what he did for revenge, wanting to avenge Mary Jane's death. Either way, it was a damn shame he had to find all this out when it was too late. But however he wanted to look at it, the thing was, it was too late and there were more pressing matters to worry about, now. The result being that DJ was dead and he was still alive and planned on staying that way for the foreseeable future.

"What do we do?" Matt asked to whoever wanted to answer him.

"I have no idea, pal, but just stay still and don't make any fast moves," Bubba said in a low voice. "Maybe they'll leave us alone. Shit, maybe DJ took the fight out of them."

Then there was the sound of claws on wood and it was coming from the opposite side of the three foot wall. At first the five survivors didn't move, not understanding what they were hearing. Behind them, the roof door shook again, but held and the noise was muffling the new scratching sound.

But then the noise made itself known when over the top of the wall, coming from the outside of the diner, more than two score small rodents and climbing animal's swarmed onto the roof, causing some of the birds to take flight. The animals had taken the outside wall of the diner as the path of least resistance and were now attacking en masse, the five survivors now trapped on the roof with nowhere to go. The remaining birds fluttered their wings and when the first of the rodents were on the roof, the birds took flight, joining their brethren, all heading straight for the five humans.

Matt ducked low and reached out for a piece of plywood, the two foot by two foot square, flat piece of wood resembling a makeshift shield. He had Liz get behind him and he used the wood like a shield, but also like a weapon, smacking birds out of the air like he was whacking fruit tossed to him by an unruly child. Bubba had found a large piece of sheet metal, only his large bulk able to wield the metal at all. Jake would have been hard pressed to do the same.

With a mighty roar, Bubba raised the sheet metal slab over his head and then fanned the air with it, slapping birds to the roof where he then stepped on them with his already bloody and gore covered boots.

Beth had found a twisted piece of rebar about four feet long and she used it like a spear, stabbing the rodents that came towards her. Possums, rats, mice, anything that could climb were scurrying onto the roof, wanting to taste the flesh of the humans.

The battle went on long into the night, the undead menace never faltering. But in time, even the animals slowed, like the outgoing tide, the swarm thinned and soon there was nothing left on the roof but twitching carcasses and crimson and torn fur. The roof was bathed in blood, sometimes an inch thick and the patrons splashed as they moved about the roof. In time they spread out, standing at the three foot wall and slapping any animals that tried to climb over. They were like ancient warriors holding their fort, under siege by an army of the dead, and they fought valiantly, knowing to stop, to even slow their defense, would mean death to one or all. In time they were able to let one of them rest, the other four having to battle harder to take up the slack. The night turned to day and soon it was afternoon again, the amber sky an ominous picture of death above them. Still the animals came, more birds appeared, bald eagles, and small sparrows which were caught in hands and crushed, their small carcasses dropped to the roof where dozens more were already piled high. Crows, seagulls and pigeons by the dozens attacked again and again and only Bubba's indomitable will saved the others time and again. The birds couldn't penetrate the large metal slab and were slapped out of the sky like the hand of God had been angered and had reached down from Heaven to smite the dead beasts. But if God was in play, he was remaining silent, the five survivors knowing they were on their own. There would be no rescue, and as the hours wore on to the second night on the roof, they knew there would be no help from anyone but themselves.

In one of the lulls of battle, the animals themselves seeming to be regrouping, Beth and Jake had a chance to talk. While they talked, Bubba strolled around the roof, stepping on anything that still twitched. The gore was a foot high in places and the smell, and the flies were unbelievable, the redolence of death a palpable thing, like an early morning fog coming in off the harbor.

There were thousands of flies, and maggots were everywhere, crawling in and out of the dead flesh, a banquet of unimaginable bounty. Jake wondered where all the blood had come from. If most of the animals were already dead, then why was there so much blood? Shaking his head, he knew some answers would never be answered, so what was the point in asking.

"Why did this happen?" Beth asked him, wiping her face with her shirt. The gesture was silly as her shirt was covered in animal gore. Still, Jake thought she looked beautiful; her large brown eyes catching the moonlight and reflecting it back to him.

Jake shrugged. "Who knows? Sometimes shit just happens. There's no reason for it. It just happens. You can try to give it a reason, but in the end there isn't one. Some people can't accept that, though, and that's why they get killed."

"You mean I should just accept that dead animals are trying to kill me and then go have a cup of coffee and a cigarette?" She smiled crookedly, her nose scrunching up and Jake felt his heart skip a beat.

He shook his head, his hair matted to his scalp and covered in blood. A few feathers stuck to his forehead and Beth reached out and plucked them away. He smiled, thanking her and answered her question.

"No, of course not. But if you try to think about it too closely, all you're gonna do is go crazy. Take that little guy in the diner. The little bastard just got up and went to the doors and opened them. Hell, I have to wonder if he even knew what he was doing."

"He must have, or else why would he do it?"

"That's a good question and maybe one of us will get the chance to ask him one day in Heaven, but hopefully not today."

Beth looked up at the moon and clouds, the billowing mass sometimes blocking the moonlight until the wind carried them away. Then the round orb would reappear like a giant eye watching them from above. It was ominous, staring up into that sky, wondering what the next hour would bring.

"Are we gonna live through this, Jake?" She asked, tears welling up in the corner of her eyes. "I don't want to die. I've got so much to see and so much I want to do. Hell, I haven't even been to Florida for Spring Break. How can I die without doing that?"

"Yeah, I know what you mean. I've never been out of New Hampshire."

She sniffed and smiled wanly. "You're kidding. Not even once? What about Boston? It's not that far."

He shook his head. "Nope, afraid not. Born here and I guess I'll probably die here." He spit a wad of saliva onto the roof and cleared his throat. "I just hope that won't be today."

She took a step closer to him and leaned forward, turning her head slightly. Before she kissed him, she wiped his lips with her finger, not wanting to get any blood on her mouth. Then they kissed, sweet and soft. When she leaned back, Jake was still leaning forward, his eyes still closed.

"Okay, lover boy, we're done," she said softly.

He opened his eyes, blinked once and then a sly grin crossed his face. "Huh? Oh, sorry, yeah I guess we are."

The entire conversation and kiss had taken less than three minutes and now that they were separated, Bubba let out a yell from across the roof.

"Here they come again, boys and girls. Grab your cocks, hold your balls and get ready to fight!"

Beth picked up the rebar, the bar feeling like it weighed a ton, her arms were so sore. Jake reached down and picked up his blood-red two-by-four. His hands were so full of blisters he could barely hold it and he had more splinters than he could count; thanks to swinging the wood around like a club without gloves.

Matt and Liz did the same, Liz now holding a small garbage can lid, one of the old metal ones. Bubba had found it while he was making sure the defeated animals were truly dead. The lid was perfect for the small woman, as Liz was no taller than five feet with a petite form. But the woman had a fighter's spirit and used the lid like a shield, and sometimes as an offensive weapon, battering the animals to the roof, where she would step on the lid, squashing the inside of the animals to mush. The lid was stained maroon with splashes of fresh red and she looked like a tiny Amazon princess. Matt was no better, covered from head to toe in gore. His eyes peeked out from behind his red-splattered face like a pygmy hiding in the brush, and his brown hair seemed to be painted onto his scalp. With Bubba's yell, he jumped to his feet and turned to face the next onslaught. More than three score attackers swarmed over the roof wall and though the amount of birds had dwindled, more than a hundred dove out of the night sky, with only blood on their tiny minds.

The battle was joined again and the five survivors defended their lives with renewed fury.

For to acquiesce, to hesitate for more than a moment, would be a fate worse than death.

* * *

The night passed fitfully, the undead swarm coming and going with each passing hour and it was with heavy and weary hearts that the five battered diner survivors greeted the slowly rising dawn. Clouds had gathered in the sky late in the night and with the overcast horizon, the yellow waves of the comet could barely be seen. Not that there was much time for gazing up at the sky with their lives in a constant state of danger. Dark pillars of smoke could be seen rising in the distance, most likely coming from Portsmouth, but the far away city was of no consequence as the here and now took precedent.

The animals had been regrouping again, gathering in numbers in the parking lot in the front and back of the diner, and as the five humans walked to the edge of the roof, their feet a foot deep in animal gore, they gazed down at the parking lot. More dead animals were coming out of the tree line, dragging their decomposing carcasses across the pavement, all heading for the diner. The five people were the only ones left in a ten mile radius and all the undead beasts wanted a piece of their tender flesh.

"Holy shit, is that Carlos?" Jake asked, looking down at the dead dishwasher who had just exited the destroyed diner. The body was barely human, Jake could see, as the man shambled out into the open, having survived the fatal explosion inside the diner. Well, he sort of survived.

Carlos's head was almost severed from his shoulders, hanging over his back like he had been punched in the nose and his head had snapped back like a Jack-in-the-Box. His abdomen and chest was a gaping, jagged hole and his left arm was missing, severed at the shoulder, fractured bone peeking out the end like a sharp blade. His right leg was bent at an unnatural angle, his tibia jutting through the exposed flesh, and he dragged it while he stumbled around the parking lot. In the night, the darkness hiding shapes and shadows, Jake hadn't seen his old friend until the sky began to lighten ever so slightly.

The zombie wobbled around on unsteady legs and then he seemed to realize he was being watched. Turning to the side, his one remaining eye looking up at Jake, Carlos used his remaining hand to flip him off.

Jake blinked, unable to believe what he was seeing.

"Jesus Christ. Not only do they become zombies, but they turn into assholes, too."

Beth chuckled then, a spat of the giggles taking over her. Jake smirked back, not realizing he had said anything amusing until she began to chuckle louder.

He looked up at the sky at the circling birds and then he turned to Bubba.

"When do you think they'll come at us again?"

"Don't know, Jake, but shit, there can't be much more of 'em."

"They'll never stop coming. At least not until we're all dead," Liz mumbled from his side. Bubba turned and looked down at the blood-splattered woman.

"You might be right, miss, but I'll tell you this. I still got some fight left in me and I got this, too." He pulled the gun out of his pants. "If it looks like things are going bad, I already made sure to save five bullets for us."

Liz stared at the gun and then her lip quivered. She turned away and fell into Matt's arms, crying. Matt looked up at Bubba while he hugged his wife, the trucker more than a foot taller than him, and he nodded, knowing the big trucker had the right idea. Better a bullet in the head than to become a walking corpse.

"Christ, Bubba, way to give a pep talk," Jake quipped, frowning as he stared down at Carlos. The zombie had turned away now and was trying to organize the animals for their last push at the humans on the diner's roof. He was like a battalion general ordering his troops into formation and it was a strange sight indeed, if that could be possible.

"Sorry, Jake, but it's the truth. I don't see any reason to toss bullshit around, especially at a time like this. I don't want to die, but if it's a bullet or becoming like him," he gestured to Carlos, "well, I'll take the bullet anytime."

"Why? For all we know, Carlos is happy like that," Beth said, though she didn't really believe what she was saying.

Bubba looked down on her, opened his mouth like he was going to answer her, then closed it, lips smacking shut.

"Too easy," he said and then walked away, moving a few feet to his right to see what was happening on the opposite side of the roof.

Beth watched the trucker walk away and then she turned back to Jake. Jake was grinning, his teeth whiter against his blood-splattered face and Beth raised her eyebrows, then lowered them when she realized he was laughing at her, not with her.

"Well, maybe he is," she said, trying to defend her statement.

"Hey, whatever, maybe we'll get the chance to find out," Jake said.

"You might get that chance sooner than you think, Jake," Matt said, askance of him. "Here they come again and there's a lot more than before!"

All eyes turned to where Matt was looking and mouths opened in gasps of shock. More than five hundred birds had landed on the nearby telephone wires surrounding the diner and hundreds upon hundreds of dead creatures were spilling forth from the tree line. Badgers, possums, deer, rats, dogs, housecats, and a few ferrets to keep things interesting, were all slowly crawling out of the forest. As the five humans watched, none could believe their eyes.

"Good God, they must be coming from miles in every direction," Matt said as he eyed a large Bull Moose with half a head and a large hole in its side he could see clear through.

Jake took a step backward and reached out for Beth's hand. He knew there would be no way of fending off that many animals and birds. The odds were simply against them; no matter how determined they were to survive.

He decided he needed to say something to Beth and now was the last chance he was going to get, so spinning on his heels, he grabbed her by the cheeks and stared into her eyes.

"I need to tell you something and you need to listen. We only have a few seconds. You understand?"

She nodded, tried to say something and he squeezed her cheeks harder, cutting her off. She squeaked, but remained silent. Behind Jake, the dead birds fluttered dry wings, preparing to attack. Beth found it very hard to focus on Jake with her impending doom hanging over her head like a large pendulum.

"I love you." He hesitated for an instant and then continued. "Now, I know it sounds crazy, I know we just met, but the instant I saw you, I just knew it. You don't have to say anything; I just wanted you to know that again." He let go of her cheeks and she nodded.

"Jake I ..." And that was all she could say as the predawn was blocked by the massive flock of birds which had taken flight from their perches and were now on the move. Crows, pigeons, sparrows, robins, sea gulls, all types and sizes and shapes were in this menagerie of avian death and they were all heading for the five humans. Below, on the ground, the animals that could crawl were on the move, only a few yards from the diner's buckled walls, the grenades having weakened the foundation. Which the large moose and bear used to their advantage, entering the diner and plowing into the stanchions which supported the roof. With each crash of the solid and undead bodies, the diner would shake slightly, threatening to bring the entire structure down in a cave-in of ash and destruction.

The five humans backed up, placing shoulder blades against one another, hoping that by doing such a thing they could last even longer, hopefully preventing any creatures from attacking from behind.

Then Jake looked up into the sky, the first bird gazing down at him, a malevolence in its eyes that was as unearthly as the comet in orbit over the Earth.

"Good luck, guys," Bubba said as he fingered his handgun with his free hand. The last load of rounds was in it and he could only fire a few shots before saving the last bullets for him and the others. He had already planned how it would go. First Liz would get it, then Matt. Then Beth and Jake, followed by him swallowing the muzzle. That would be the hardest and he prayed he had the willpower to squeeze the trigger on himself.

"Yeah, Bubba, you, too," Jake said. "It's been a blast."

Weapons were raised and the five warriors prepared for their final battle, just as the sun broke through the clouds, bathing the new day with its golden brilliance. But there was something different about this sky.

Where the sky had been an amber hue, now it was replaced with an azure blue, the comet finally passing the Earth and moving on deeper into the Milky Way to orbit around the sun and return in two hundred years.

Just as the first avian prepared to dive at the survivors and the first rodents and climbing beasts reached the rooftop, the radiation or strange anomaly breathing false life into them evaporated like smoke on the wind.

Like a light switch had been turned off, every creature stopped moving, then collapsed to the rooftop, or fell off the diner wall, or dropped to the pavement, dead once again. The only problem for Jake and the others were all the animated birds, now dead once again, plummeted out of the sky like feathered bricks. Hundreds of birds fell like hard rain, the five survivors running back and forth doing their best to somehow avoid being struck. Jake took more than a few blows to the head, but the avians weren't that heavy and he survived with a few small wounds where beaks and claws had caught his flesh. Carlos' body leaned back, so his swinging head could look up at the sky, his eyes already doing the same thing, and his mouth opened wide in anguish. Then the body toppled over to lay still, the life draining out of the mangled limbs forever.

On the roof, the birds finished their fall, and their carcasses filled the rooftop two feet deep.

Climbing over the birds, the five people moved back to the edge of the roof, gazing out over the parking lot.

Nothing moved, only the wind stirring the fur of the creatures. The stench of death was overwhelming and it was all any of them could do to not to vomit. Liz lost that battle and spewed forth her insides across a pile of crows and pigeons. Once finished, she still felt terrible and Bubba slapped Jake on the arm, pointing to the roof access door.

"I don't know if it's safe or not. But I think we should take this chance and get off this roof. My rig is down there and we can get in it and get the hell out of here."

"Sound good to me, let's go," Jake said.

With Beth by his side, Jake made his way over the piles of birds and other animals, his feet sinking up to his calves and sometimes over his shins. Every step was a work of torture, the squishing and squirting of the small carcasses spewing filth everywhere. Sometimes the fluid would shoot straight up, dance in the sunlight to then fall back down. It was a hard walk, crossing the ten yards to the door, but soon they were there and one at a time made their way back down to ground level. Bubba was first, and with handgun leading the way, he pushed through the debris and into the diner. The moose and bears were lying on their sides, and warily, Bubba moved over and poked one with the barrel of his gun. Pleased to see them inanimate, he waved the others to come out of the stairwell.

"I don't know what the hell's going on, but I think it might be over."

"Well, let's not wait around to find out," Jake said as he stepped into the diner. The place looked like a war zone, blasted and burned walls and glass everywhere. Body parts and bits of DJ lined the corners of the room and Jake saw DJ's hat lying nearby. Reaching over, he picked it up, then smacked it on his leg. It was blood splattered, but had made it through the explosion relatively intact. He tried it on and smiled at Beth. She shook her head no and with a frown he took it off. He tossed it onto the dead moose and the five of them moved out to the parking lot.

All expected the animals to jump up at any moment, as if it was some sort of ingenious trap, set in motion to get them off the roof, but with each passing second, they could see that wasn't the case.

Crossing the carcass-strewn parking lot, Bubba reached his rig, and with a whoop of laughter, climbed into the cab and fired up the engine. The motor roared to life, and he blew the air horn, while smoke billowed out the exhaust pipe. Matt and Liz turned away, and with a wave to Jake and Beth, began walking to their car parked five spots away from the semi.

"We have our own car and we'll be going too. I'm not waiting around for things to change back again, so thanks for everything and I wish you luck, both of you," Matt said. Liz nodded that she agreed with her husband.

Jake and Beth waved. "Yeah, I understand, go, and good luck to you, wherever you go next," Jake said.

Matt nodded, waved one last time and with Liz's hand in his, the couple ran for their car. In seconds they were inside, the motor turned over and the car was screeching out of the parking lot, the tires churning up the animal carcasses in the wheel wells as the car sped out onto the highway and headed for the interstate.

Bubba blew his air horn again and Matt did the same with his car's horn. Gunning the engine, Bubba leaned out to Jake and Beth, the motor settling into a soporific hum.

"You two coming or what?"

"Yeah, Bubba, just give me a sec, all right?" Bubba frowned, but he leaned back inside the cab. A second later, Waylon Jennings could be heard, blasting over the parking lot.

"You think it's really over?" Beth asked Jake as she stared at the carcasses and Carlos' dead and mangled corpse lying across the pavement. Then she gazed up at the deep blue sky. The clouds had cleared it looked like it was going to be a beautiful day.

"Seems to be, though I still can't believe it happened in the first place. It's still hard to believe and I was there, you now?" Jake said, while scratching his head. The blood was drying on his skin and it itched something awful.

"Yeah, but here's something to think on," Beth told him. "Could it happen again? I mean, when the comet comes back, and that of course is assuming I was right and all this is because of that comet, will all this just happen all over again?"

Jake gave her words a second's thought and then shook his head, pushing them from his mind.

"You know what, Beth? Let the people in the future worry about it. I mean, it's too far away for us to even think of dealing with it, right? We'll make sure to teach our kids and get them ready for what will happen when the comet returns. Yeah, let's let our kids deal with it. As for now, we have each other and the future."

"Our kids? Getting a little ahead of yourself aren't you, Jake? Man, you are so corny sometimes, you know that?" Beth said with a grin.

Jake grinned back, "Yeah, I know, but sometimes corny's good, isn't it."

"Yeah, I guess you're right," she said. She quirked her head to the right. "It has its places."

"You know, back on the roof, when I told you I love you, you were gonna say something back to me, but you got cut off. Care to tell me now?" Jake asked with hope in his voice.

Waylon Jennings howled to the world, Bubba singing along off key.

With a sigh she shook her head. "Men, you are so obtuse sometimes."

She stepped so close to him he could smell her breath and see the freckles on her face under the blood splatter. Before he could say a thing, she leaned in to him, kissing him hard and passionately. The kiss lingered, her tongue touching his, searching and probing. When she finally stepped away, his mouth was hanging open, his eyes wide.

"Does that answer your question?" She asked, coyly.

He nodded slowly, speechless from the kiss.

"Hey you two, suck face on your own time. Let's get the hell out of here already!" Bubba yelled and stepped on the gas, the massive engine roaring with power as it idled.

With a grin, Jake reached out and took her hand, the two of them moving around to the passenger side of the rig, Beth going in first, followed by Jake.

When the cab door was slammed closed, Bubba let out another whoop, blared the air horn and shifted the semi into first gear. With a buck and a groan, the eighteen-wheeler began to move, crunching over carcasses and spewing organs and gore in all directions, leaving flattened corpses in its wake.

"So where are we gonna go now?" Beth asked. "For all we know, what happened here is still going on. You saw that smoke coming from the city."

Bubba nodded. "Maybe, but we got to go somewhere and I tell you what. Next time I won't be so nice. Let those dead bastards try again and you'll see what will happen."

Beth nodded, and Jake chuckled. Truth was, he didn't care where he went now, just as long as Beth was with him.

Bubba drove onto the main road, and then aimed the nose of the rig to the interstate, the horn sounding one last time.

Then the truck was moving at a good clip and soon rose over the incline on the road and was lost from sight.

The diner was deserted now, no sounds could be heard and nothing stirred. But the foundation was weakened to the point of collapse and as the semi disappeared down the road, the structure succumbed to all the abuse it had received and collapsed, caving in on itself in large crunch of steel, metal and stone.

When the dust settled, all was silent for some time, but soon a small hole under the counter showed a stirring of life. The Formica counter had protected the small hole from damage and inside was a small mouse. No more than two inches big, the small rodent sniffed the air, unsure if it was safe to finally leave its hiding place. It had been hiding for days, too petrified of the unnatural creatures above and the constant activity of the humans who had never left the diner at night like before.

But soon it took a chance and crawled out into the light of day.

This was a living, breathing mouse, one that had stayed hidden, sensing the unnatural rodents above would have killed it the instant they found it. Now sensing the danger had passed, it moved deeper into the diner, already thinking about finding some small crumbs of sustenance to fill its empty belly.

The other rodent carcasses around it remained immobile, finally dead once again, and that was fine with the mouse, pleased the natural state of life had finally been restored. And so the mouse began foraging for food in the destroyed diner as the sun rose overhead on a beautiful new day, casting the land in a golden halo of gorgeous majesty and hope.

The following is a bonus short story by the author

It Was Just A Dream

Tom's eyes snapped open and he rolled over on the couch, his face now sinking into the plush material.

Turning his head so he could breathe, he opened his eyes and stared up at the ceiling.

His heart was beating in his chest and he could feel perspiration crawling down his back and saturating his clothing.

Wow, he thought, *that had been some dream.*

He was still wearing the jeans and polo shirt from the day before, the mustard stain from the hotdog he'd had at lunch still prevalent on his chest. The Nike sneakers he had bought at Footlocker a week ago for 79.99 were still on his feet, too, the laces still tied.

The room was dark, all the shades drawn, and he held up his right arm to check his wrist watch. The luminous dial told him it was three a.m.

He barely registered the fact there was no sound coming from outside his windows. Usually, there would be the constant cacophony of traffic, horns beeping and motors racing, but in his fugue-like state, he didn't notice there was only silence.

He felt a kink in his back, so he stretched, trying to push the images of his dream from his mind.

And what a dream it was.

In his dream, the dead had begun to walk, as ridiculous as that would seem. And the dream had been so vivid. He clearly could remember his fright and shock of watching the first shambling corpses stroll down Main St., the first one with a toe tag on her arm and a large V on her torso from her autopsy.

Tom recalled she was strikingly beautiful, with long, golden tresses and a trim figure, though a little pasty for his taste. Perhaps she could go to the tanning salon?

Just because she was dead didn't mean she couldn't still look good. He remembered how her face had sagged to the right and the left eye had curved upward, though the face was still attractive.

Then in his dream, he was distracted by the next ghoul he had seen. A few feet behind the blonde zombie, a headless man walked along like he was going for a Sunday stroll.

His head was still with him, however, only now it was in a paper bag in the man's left hand. While the dead man walked, the bag swung bag and forth to the rhythm of his stride, a few spots of blood dripping onto the street from the bottom of the bag as he went. There was a toe tag on this animated corpse, too. And there was a brief description of an automobile accident and a decapitation on the tag, scrawled out in the coroner's messy, stilted handwriting.

The next ghoul in line was small and was a little girl. She had red and blue marks on her neck from where she had been strangled, after being ruthlessly raped and murdered. In her right arm she hugged the dolly that had been her safety blanket for most of her young life.

Unfortunately, the dolly hadn't protected her from the monster of a neighbor who had lived next door to her and had secretly watched her while she played in the backyard with her dolls. Then one night, only two days ago, he had acted on his impulses and had taken a young life not meant for the realm of death just yet.

Tom could only stand in the street, mouth agape, as the young ghoul shambled down the sidewalk, her plodding footsteps making her look like she was sleepwalking. It was only when Tom saw the milky white dead eyes that he realized she wasn't alive, but truly dead.

Arriving after getting a call about a naked woman and a headless man, a policeman had pulled his squad car over, jumping out with nightstick in hand. He had gone over to the ghouls, wanting to stop the naked corpse from strolling down Main Street.

Not understanding the full extent of what was happening; he only assumed it was some sort of prank, or perhaps a college initiation gone too far.

He chose the naked ghoul first as there was a public nudity law in effect and she would need to get some clothes on or risk going to jail.

When the cop moved closer and saw those dead eyes and autopsy scar on her chest, his mouth dropped open and he began to stutter. Reaching for his radio, he called in to the station about the odd looking woman, and when he saw the headless corpse behind her, he dropped the radio and took a step backwards. On instinct, he drew his service revolver, aiming it at the headless corpse.

In the decapitated body's hand, the paper bag had ripped open, the still moving dead eyes of the severed head glaring back at the officer.

Shouting a warning, and frankly not having a clue what he should do, the policeman opened fire on the headless copse, round after round striking the center of the ghoul's chest.

The heavy .38's ripped into the ghoul, shattering organs and fracturing ribs. The front of the headless corpse didn't look that bad, only a few holes to show where the rounds had entered the body, but it was on the rear of the ghoul where the true damage was obvious. Large, fist sized holes had appeared as if by magic, the bullets exploding outward, shredding the body like it had been dropped into a blender. Gobbets of flesh and gore bathed the street, splattering the road with crimson. The blood was slow, syrupy, the plasma slowly congealing now that the owner of the viscous fluid was dead.

Behind the headless ghoul, the little girl was splashed with red, small dots appearing on her gaunt face like tiny freckles. Her dolly received an ample dose of gore, as well; chunks of viscera landing on the dolly to slide off and fall to the pavement with wet splashy sounds.

But the cop had been concentrating too much on the headless ghoul and had let his guard down on the naked woman. Before he realized it, she was on him, her teeth sinking into his forearm, ripping his uniform sleeve and a large chunk of his flesh to boot. He screamed, dropping his revolver and panicked, pushing the woman off him. Reaching down, he pulled his nightstick off his belt, after holstering it before pulling his revolver. The nightstick cracked over the naked ghoul's head, leaving a large indent in her forehead. Her head turned with the blow, but as the cop watched, her head slowly turned back to face him, her mouth and chin now coated a dark scarlet from his blood.

Vermillion ribbons sluiced down her chest, sliding between her once shapely breasts, now deformed thanks to the autopsy scar, then continued on to the dark hair between her groin. Despite his terror, the officer noticed the carpet did not match the drapes, but then he was backing away from her, his wounded arm out, his other hand swinging the nightstick for all he was worth.

The naked ghoul hissed, blood shooting from her mouth like she was spitting, then she lunged for him. He swatted her with the nightstick, the tip striking the woman's left eye socket, puncturing the white orb within, but the ghoul never slowed.

Tom stared at the tableaux end of the street, watching helplessly as the naked woman fell on top of the cop and began sinking her teeth into the side of his neck. Even from his distance away, Tom saw the blood fountain arch upward, then fall back to the ground like rain as the ghoul severed the man's jugular with her teeth. Then the small girl was with the naked ghoul and they both began feeding on the hapless policeman.

In less than two minutes, the cop's kicking legs faltered and he laid still, the two ghouls continuing to feed. The headless corpse shambled up and the body leaned over, allowing the severed head to try and take a bite of the cop's twitching body. Chewing bits of bloody meat, the pulped flesh slid out the bottom of the neck, to splatter onto the sidewalk.

The head didn't care, of course, and went in for more.

Tom continued to stare, mouth hanging slack, blinking continually as he watched at the visceral scene of death only a few dozen feet away.

Then, coming around the far corner, he saw more people, more shambling forms slowly moving towards him. At first his legs wouldn't move, and no matter how hard he tried, he couldn't run away. In his dream, he screamed to himself to run, to get away before he joined the cop in a dismembered death.

A moaning sound filled his ears, a despairing wailing that filled the soul with hopelessness and loss, and of pain and suffering. Tom realized the sound was coming from the treacle-like people moving towards him.

Then he snapped out of his stupor and his legs were free!

Like they had been incased in ice and then the block shattered, his legs were free to run. And so he did, all the way back home.

Slamming his front door, he had sat down on his couch in a daze, unable to believe what he had been witness to, the dream flowing like a movie on a giant screen.

His mind refused to accept the utter unbelievably of what he had seen, and he shook his head again and again, as if that gesture alone could change the facts.

Ten minutes later, the first sounds of a city falling apart came to his ears. It was an explosion across town, the pillars of smoke drifting into the sky to blend with the clouds, tainting the once blue horizon gray. Then the sounds of crunching metal could be heard; two cars fornicating as they strike each other head on, bodies going head first through windshields to fall in a tangle of limbs on the warm asphalt of the road.

Gunshots filtered into his head, some of the citizens fighting back, but soon, they too, would evaporate, becoming less and less noticeable as the day wore on.

Tom wondered where his roommate was. Will should be home by now and surely with everything that was happening; he would have left work, wanting to reach the safety of his home.

In his dream, Tom felt weary and laid his head down, falling asleep from stress and exhaustion.

And now he stood up, the room was still very dark and he realized the shades were drawn on every window. The house was silent and he went to the bathroom, splashed some water on his face as he tried to wash the images of death and destruction away from his mind. The bathroom light didn't work which was odd, but there was just enough light from the moon outside to filter through the drawn shades.

Finishing up, he went back into the living room and stood quietly with hands on his hips as he stared at the darkened room.

It was then that Will stepped out of the kitchen to see Tom was awake. He carried a candle in his hand, the pale glow giving his face a pallid look. The man looked haggard, as if he had been worried about something. His clothes were torn in a few places and there were a few stains of red on his shirt. Tom assumed the man had spilled ketchup on himself, the man notoriously sloppy when he was eating.

Will stepped into the living room and set the candle down on a small end table, then dropped onto the couch.

"Good, you're up," he said. "When I came home earlier, I thought I'd just leave you alone. It's good to see you made it, too. How're you feeling? It's some crazy shit going on, huh?"

Tom didn't know what he was talking about, but he nodded.

"Yeah, guess so. I tell you, I had the craziest dream, you wouldn't believe me if I told you."

Will only bent his head to the right, gesturing for Tom to go on.

"Try me, after the past day I think I would believe anything," Will said.

Tom was about to open his mouth, to share with Will the crazy dream he had of dead people walking and a world fallen into chaos when there was a pounding on the front door, the staccato beat like a bass drum.

"Good God, who the hell is beating on our door like that?" Tom said angrily, turning and walking to the door in one smooth motion, his hand already reaching out to unlock the door and give the person on the other side a piece of his mind.

Will's eyes went wide with shock as he watched Tom reach out for the doorknob.

"Wait, Tom, what the hell are you doing! Don't open that door, you'll kill us both!"

But Tom wasn't listening, too wrapped up in what he was going to say to the jerk that was pounding on his door.

Opening the door, with Will's words echoing in his ears, Tom prepared his retort to the intruder opposite his front door, the epitaph already lodged in his throat. Before he could do or say anything, however, multiple bloody, claw-like hands reached out and grabbed him, yanking him through the doorway and away from the safety of his home. He screamed when his hair was pulled from his scalp and a dozen hands ripped at his clothing. Snarling faces looked down on his, and he felt himself forced to the ground. Then, just before the first set of blood-red jaws descended over his face, blocking out his surrounding's; he let out one bloodcurdling exclamation, his words intertwined into the scream like a mantra.

"No! No! It was just a dream! It was just a dream!"

Then mind-numbing pain filled his mind and he was lost in a sea of anguish and agony, while outside on the street, the city burned, the flames engulfing everything.

And while Tom was having his insides torn from his body, devoured by the hungry masses of the undead; shadowy, shambling forms swarmed through the metropolis, consuming everything in their path.

DEAD RECKONING: DAWNING OF THE DEAD
By Anthony Giangregorio

THE DEAD HAVE RISEN!

In the dead city of Pittsburgh, two small enclaves struggle to survive, eking out an existence of hand to mouth.

But instead of working together, both groups battle for the last remaining fuel and supplies of a city filled with the living dead.

Six months after the initial outbreak, a lone helicopter arrives bearing two more survivors and a newborn baby. One enclave welcomes them, while the other schemes to steal their helicopter and escape the decaying city.

With no police, fire, or social services existing, the two will battle for dominance in the steel city of the walking dead.

But when the dust settles, the question is: will the remaining humans be the winners, or the losers?

When the dead walk, the line between Heaven and Hell is so twisted and bent there is no line at all.

RISE OF THE DEAD
By Anthony Giangregorio

DEATH IS ONLY THE BEGINNING

In less than forty-eight hours, more than half the globe was infected.

In another forty-eight, the rest would be enveloped.

The reason?

A science experiment gone horribly wrong which enabled the dead to walk, their flesh rotting on their bones even as they seek human prey.

Jeremy was an ordinary nineteen year old slacker. He partied too much and had done poorly in high school. After a night of drinking and drugs, he awoke to find the world a very different place from the one he'd left the night before.

The dead were walking and feeding on the living, and as Jeremy stepped out into a world gone mad, the dead spotting him alone and unarmed in the middle of the street, he had to wonder if he would live long enough to see his twentieth birthday.

BOOK 6

DEAD UNION
By Anthony Giangregorio

BRAVE NEW WORLD

More than a year has passed since the world died not with a bang, but with a moan.
Where sprawling cities once stood, now only the dead inhabit the hollow walls of a shattered civilization; a mockery of lives once led.
But there are still survivors in this barren world, all slowly struggling to take back what was stripped from their birthright; the promise of a world free of the undead.
Fortified towns have shunned the outside world, becoming massive fortresses in their own right. These refugees of a world torn asunder are once again trying to carve out a new piece of the earth, or hold onto what little they already possess.

HOSTAGES

Henry Watson and his warrior survivalists are conscripted by a mad colonel, one of the last military leaders still functioning in the decimated United States. The colonel has settled in Fort Knox, and from there plans to rule the world with his slave army of lost souls and the last remaining soldiers of a defunct army.
But first he must take back America and mold it in his own image; and he will crush all who oppose him, including the new recruits of Henry and crew.
The battle lines are drawn with the fate of America at stake, and this time, the outcome may be unsure.
In a world where the dead walk, even the grave isn't safe

THE DARK
By Anthony Giangregorio

DARKNESS FALLS

The darkness came without warning.

First New York, then the rest of United States, and then the world became enveloped in a perpetual night without end.

With no sunlight, eventually the planet will wither and die, bringing on a new Ice Age. But that isn't problem for the human race, for humanity will be dead long before that happens.

There is something in the dark, creatures only seen in nightmares, and they are on the prowl.

Evolution has changed and man is no longer the dominant species.

When we are children, we are told not to fear the dark, that what we believe to exist in the shadows is false.

Unfortunately, that is no longer true.

ANOTHER EXCITING CHAPTER IN THE DEADWATER SERIES!

DEADRAIN
By Anthony Giangregorio

Welcome to the New America, population: 0

When a bacterial outbreak contaminates America's lower atmosphere, the resulting rain mutates into a deadly conduit for death.

Human's all over America are exposed and within a matter of days society has crumbled and the walking dead rule the land.

The America we know is gone, replaced by a new order; where the dead walk and humans are the prey.

Henry Watson and his small group of companions travel the country, searching for someplace better, someplace where the rain is safe.

In the New America the rules have changed; survive or perish.

DARK PLACES

By Anthony Giangregorio

A cave-in inside the Boston subway unleashes something that should have stayed buried forever

Three boys sneak out to a haunted junkyard after dark and find more than they gambled on.

In a world where everyone over twelve has died from a mysterious illness, one young boy tries to carry on.

A mysterious man in black tries his hand at a game of chance at a local carnival, to interesting results.

God, Allah, and Buddha play a friendly game of poker with the fate of the Earth resting in the balance.

Ever have one of those days where everything that can go wrong, does? Well, so did Byron, and no one should have a day like this!

Thad had an imaginary friend named Charlie when he was a child. Charlie would make him do bad things. Now Thad is all grown up and guess who's coming for a visit?

These and other short stories, all filled with frozen moments of dread and wonder, will keep you captivated long into the night.

Just be sure to watch out when you turn off the light!

THE MONSTER UNDER THE BED
By Anthony Giangregorio

Rupert was just one of many monsters that inhabit the human world, scaring children before bed. Only Rupert wanted to play with the children he was forced to scare.

When Rupert meets Timmy, an instant friendship is born. Running away from his abusive step-father, Timmy leaves home, embarking on a journey that leads him to New York City.

On his way, Timmy will realize that the true monsters are other adults who are just waiting to take advantage of a small boy, all alone in the big city.

Can Rupert save him?

Or will Timmy just become another statistic.

SOULEATER
By Anthony Giangregorio

Twenty years ago, Jason Lawson witnessed the brutal death of his father by something only seen in nightmares, something so horrible he'd blocked it from his mind.

Now twenty years later the creature is back, this time for his son.

Jason won't let that happen.

He'll travel to the demon's world, struggling every second to rescue his son from its clutches.

But what he doesn't know is that the portal will only be open for a finite time and if he doesn't return with his son before it closes, then he'll be trapped in the demon's dimension forever.

DEAD TALES: SHORT STORIES TO DIE FOR
By Anthony Giangregorio

In a world much like our own, terrorists unleash a deadly dis-ease that turns people into flesh-eating ghouls.

A camping trip goes horribly wrong when forces of evil seek to dominate mankind.

After losing his life, a man returns reincarnated again and again; his soul inhabiting the bodies of animals.

In the Colorado Mountains, a woman runs for her life, stalked by a sadistic killer.

In a world where the Patriot Act has come to fruition, a man struggles to survive, despite eroding liberties.

Not able to accept his wife's death, a widower will cross into the dream realm to find her again, despite the dark forces that hold her in thrall.

These and other short stories will captivate and thrill you.

These are short stories to die for.

DEADFREEZE
By Anthony Giangregorio

THIS IS WHAT HELL WOULD BE LIKE IF IT FROZE OVER.

When an experimental serum for hypothermia goes horribly wrong, a small research station in the middle of Antarctica becomes overrun with an army of the frozen dead.

Now a small group of survivors must battle the arctic weather and a horde of frozen zombies as they make their way across the frozen plains of Antarctica to a neighboring research station.

What they don't realize is that they are being hunted by an entity whose sole reason for existing is vengeance; and it will find them wherever they run.

DEADFALL
By Anthony Giangregorio

It's Halloween in the small suburban town of Wakefield, Mass.

While parents take their children trick or treating and others throw costume parties, a swarm of meteorites enter the earth's atmosphere and crash to earth.

Inside are small parasitic worms, no larger than maggots.

The worms quickly infect the corpses at a local cemetery and so begins the rise of the undead.

The walking dead soon get the upper hand, with no one believing the truth.

That the dead now walk.

Will a small group of survivors live through the zombie apocalypse?

Or will they, too, succumb to the Deadfall.

DEAD RAGE

By
Anthony Giangregorio

An unknown virus spreads across the globe, turning ordinary people into bloodthirsty, ravenous killers.

Only a small percentage of the population is immune and soon become prey to the infected.

Amongst the infected comes a man, stricken by the virus, yet still retaining his grasp on reality. His need to destroy the *normals* becomes an obsession and he raises an army of killers to seek out and kill all who aren't *changed* like himself.

A few survivors gather together on the outskirts of Chicago and find themselves running for their lives as the specter of death looms over all.

The Dead Rage virus will find you, no matter where you hide.

Also available as The Rage Plague by Permuted Press.

LIVING DEAD PRESS

Where the Dead Walk

www.livingdeadpress.com

THE RAGE PLAGUE

A NOVEL BY ANTHONY GIANGREGORIO

An unknown virus spreads across the globe, turning ordinary people into ravenous killers. Only a small population proves to be immune, but most quickly fall prey to the infected.

Isolated on the rooftop of a school near the outskirts of Chicago, Bill Thompson and a small band of survivors come to the frightening realization that, without food or water, they will perish quickly under the hot sun. Some wish to migrate to a safer, more plentiful refuge, but the school is surrounded by rampaging murderers. Without a plan, Bill and his group don't stand a chance.

Their only hope lies in their one advantage over the infected: their ability to think.

ISBN: 978-1934861196

MONSTROUS
20 TALES OF GIANT CREATURE TERROR

Move over King Kong, there are new monsters in town! Giant beetles, towering crustaceans, gargantuan felines and massive underwater beasts, to name just a few. Think you've got what it takes to survive their attacks? Then open this baby up, and join today's hottest authors as they show us the true power of Mother Nature's creatures. With enough fangs, pincers and blood to keep you up all night, we promise you won't look at creepy crawlies the same way again.

ISBN: 978-1934861127

Permuted Press
The formula has been changed...
Shifted... Altered... *Twisted.*™

www.permutedpress.com